# Micro Moods

Amy Wilson

For John, with all my love.

# Contents

# Introduction

I started writing microfiction in late 2020 when I came across the vss (very short stories) community on Twitter. Since then, I've participated around 150 times in vss prompts, entered several flash and microfiction competitions, and been lucky enough to have a few stories published both online and in print.

The idea behind 'Micro Moods' was to take a collection of short stories, some of them based on vss tweets, some written for events such as 'National Flash Fiction Day', and some written just for this book, and to divide them into sections based on five themes: fear, melancholy, curiosity, anger, and joy.

So, whether you read this book from start to finish, or dip in and out of each section as the mood takes you, I hope that you enjoy the stories!

Amy Wilson

November 2021

# Part 1 -

# Fear

1.
The Sacrifices We Make

It was dark again when I opened up the cafe. Dark, and freezing cold. It used to be that even if there was no power at home, I could still come to the cafe to warm up, but now the power grid is down more often than not. I curse as I start the generator, but I do it quietly. We all have to make sacrifices after all, we each have to play our part.

There were new lists posted in the town square yesterday. The 'Persons of Interest' lists. The 'condemned' lists, more like. I read them for just long enough to make sure my name wasn't on it, and then for a minute or two longer so that anyone watching me would know that I was willing. That I am a patriot.

I finally managed to get the generator going, and the lights flickered into life. I turned the sign on the door to read 'Open' and then busied myself heating water.

It wasn't long before the door opened. Most people around here are early risers.

I smiled as I recognised the man in the thick, woollen overcoat.

"Hello, Matt. Coffee?"

"Unless that's illegal now too," he said.

I smiled although it wasn't funny. New prohibitions are added almost daily. Enforcement is merciless, informants are everywhere.

Everywhere.

I looked into the eyes of a man I've known almost all my life, and scrambled for the right party rhetoric.

2.
Reflections on Loneliness

I've been alone since he moved out. Lonely and alone. The nights are the worst; I can fill the days with noise and movement, but the nights hold only absence, like a shape in the bed where he used to lie.

Tonight though, something wakes me. My first thought, irrationally, is that it's him; he's come back, he's downstairs and he'll be here with me any minute. Except it couldn't be him because he threw his keys on the table, along with his wedding ring, when he left.

I grab my phone and the whole room lights up. I jump, but there's no one there. Except that I can still hear noises. I dial the emergency services and without giving them chance to finish telling me my options, I hiss, "There's someone in my house."

Part of me expects the woman on the other end of the phone line to tell me I'm just being silly. That this kind of thing only happens in movies, and I've imagined it all. Instead, she says "Can you make it out of the house?" her tone clipped and urgent.

"No," I say. I feel my entire body go cold.

Do any of the rooms in your house have a lock on the door?"

"The bathroom," I tell her, my voice shaky.

"Can you make it there?"

"Yes."

"Okay," she says. "Go, now."

I scramble from the bed, dash across the hall and into the bathroom, breathing hard as I lock the door behind me. I'm just about to speak to the operator, to let her know I made it, when I hear a noise behind me. Coming from inside the bathroom. Coming from the mirror.

Lightheaded, I peer at my reflection. Her eyes are subtly different to my own; hazel-flecked and kind. She smiles and reaches out for me. I feel the liquid cold of her glass hand close around my wrist and I know I'll never be lonely again.

3.
Demons

Alcohol. Drugs. Sex. I tried everything to pacify my demons, but nothing ever worked. I could always feel them twisting beneath my skin, clawing at me, trying to escape into the world.

The day I met you, I felt them recede, as if you'd lulled them into sleep. I knew then what you were: a pure soul. I'd never seen anything like you before, I wasn't even sure that people like you really existed.

At first, I tried to keep my distance. I was afraid that I might contaminate you somehow if I got too close. But you. You were so beautiful that you almost seemed to glow, to draw me in like nothing I've ever encountered. In the end, there was no choice for me.

We had almost a decade together. Ten years of walking hand-in-hand, of waking up curled around you every morning. And where I had been afraid that I might change you, the opposite seemed to be true – your purity was making me into a better person. You kept my demons asleep.

Last night, you didn't come home. I finally fell asleep around midnight, and I woke just after four when I heard you come in. As I woke, I felt my demons stir, stronger than ever. Why isn't this working anymore? What did you do?

4.

The Sensation of Being Watched

"I ... what was I saying?"

The woman sitting in front of him laughed. "Perhaps you've had a bit too much to drink," she suggested.

"I don't remember how I got here," Michael said, panic rising in his chest. "I don't remember who you are."

"I'll try not to be too offended," she said.

"No, really..."

"Shh." She jumped down from the stool at the breakfast bar and placed one finger on his lips. "I'm Emma. We met earlier this evening at the cocktail bar and got talking." She looked him up and down, a smile playing on her lips. "You were quite the charmer earlier," she said. "You really don't remember?"

Me? Charming? "Uh, no. I'm sorry. I really don't."

"Maybe when you sober up it'll all come back."

"I think I should probably leave."

"Oh, no, stay. Let me make you something to eat at least." She let out a self-conscious little laugh. "I feel guilty now. If I'd realised you were this drunk I never would have brought you back here, I would have put you in a taxi and sent you home."

He stood, and was about to protest when a feeling swept over him. Part hunger and part dizziness. "Whoa," he said, clutching at the back of the chair.

"Go and sit down," she said, pointing through the door to the sitting room. "I'll make you something and I'll be right in."

"Yes," he said, slowly, drawing the word out. "Okay. Thank you."

He walked slowly and with some difficulty into the

sitting room. The beige carpet was soft under his feet and the walls were painted ivory. The only artwork in the room was an image of a giant eye, its vivid green iris the only colour in a room that was otherwise almost determinedly bland. There was something unsettling about it, he decided, as he turned his back on it. Unseen, the poster blinked.

5.
Hollow Man

I must be some kind of idiot. Everyone knows to avoid this part of town. Never mind that it's the middle of the day and the sun is shining, this neighbourhood has a gloom all of its own. It's the fear. It's like a live thing here, like a parasite, leaching the joy from the air. Anybody who can afford to leave is already long gone.

But not everybody can leave and the people who remain need more help than most. It stands to reason that I would get sent here sooner or later.

I'm careful to keep my head up as I walk. Not just so that I can see anyone, anything, on the street, but so that the people who live here can see me. Can see what I am.

I'm carrying a stack of files, clutched tight to my chest, my government ID badge hanging on a lanyard, carefully visible on top of them. I must not have secured all the paperwork properly though, because a sheaf of paper is poking out of the bottom of one of the files and, before I can grab it with my free hand, it slips out and falls to the ground. I curse and reach down to pick it up.

I swear I only looked down for a second but when I raised my gaze, there he was, staring at me. A Hollow Man. Not a real person, only a ghost, an echo. My body wants to run, but then he smiles at me and there is something so real about it, so human, that I can't look away.

6.
The Man in Black

Tanner watched as the last of the fires were smothered, the process filling the air with choking, grey smoke. The initial danger had passed, but even so he shifted position, felt the heavy manacles on his ankles clank together, and watched as the guards stared grimly ahead, both of them avoiding his eyes. He would be lucky to survive the night.

The moon had risen high above the East Tower before the door opened. Tanner kept his eyes fixed on one of the guards, the younger one with the straw-coloured hair. The young man's face blanched, and he stood straighter.

The man who walked through the door paid no attention to the guards. He swept past them and crossed the room, coming to rest before Tanner.

"Well," he said. "I believe introductions are unnecessary."

Tanner looked at the man. He was so thin as to appear almost emaciated, but his clothes were well tailored and of good quality material. His pallid skin and white hair seemed almost to glow against his garb which was, from his collar down to his boots, a uniform shade of black.

Tanner realised that the man was waiting for an answer. He gave a quick nod.

"Very good," the man said. "That will at least save us some time."

His voice was soft in the way that distant thunder is soft; it had an underlying note of menace.

"If you know who I am then you also know why it would be unwise for you to lie to me."

Tanner nodded. He had heard the stories. They all had.

"Then we will begin with a simple question. Did you have prior knowledge of the attack?"

Desperate to avoid an outright lie, Tanner grasped for a version of the truth that might save him.

"I had some limited information," he admitted. "Although I had not yet verified its accuracy."

"And yet you chose not to share that information with your superiors. I would say that places a large portion of the blame for this event on your head."

Tanner closed his eyes. There was no need for further discussion. Sentence had already been passed.

7.
Decoy

You used your sadness like a decoy to lure me in. You told me all about your unhappy childhood, all about your parents. Their drinking.

"You're the only one who ever believed in me," you said. "You're the only good thing in my life."

Your pain seemed to call out to me, to speak to the part of me that just wanted to make everything better. The part of me that just wanted to help.

"You always make me feel better," you said, hugging me close.

And then, once I was thoroughly caught and settled into the idea that I could heal you, the tears dried up and left only anger in their wake.

"You're always trying to undermine me," you said, the first time you hit me. "Meeting you is my biggest regret."

Your rage frightened me, and your pleasure in my fear was what bothered me the most. It humiliated me, isolating me until I had no one to turn to for help.

"You always make me feel like shit," you said, pushing me away.

8.
Miss. Trust

Your first mistake was believing in me.

It's understandable I suppose. I certainly seem trustworthy enough. I dress well – nothing flashy, nothing designer, but nicely enough. My hair is always neat, my makeup is understated but immaculately applied. I'm articulate, well-spoken, and polite. You think you like me.

You don't know me.

I'm the one who's always just on the periphery of the conversation. Smiling, encouraging, offering the occasional anecdote, without ever revealing anything too personal. A smiling stranger on a train. A colleague who you've worked with for years without ever really getting to know. Someone who's never given you any reason to distrust them.

You'll never see me coming.

9.
The Masks We Wear

The room was filled with costumes. Robes hung from rails near the ceiling, shoes spilled from boxes on the floor, and wigs had been crammed onto every shelf.

But it was the masks that drew her attention. Every possible space on the wall had a mask attached to it. There were carved wooden masks and cheap rubber ones. Smiling, frowning, their features contorted in horror or frozen in rage. She looked over each one.

"Be careful with your choice," the man said. "Consider the face you wish to present to the world."

His own face seemed to shift as she looked at him, as if his features were in flux.

"You promised I could choose one to keep," she reminded him, trying not to sound petulant.

In answer, he merely indicated the walls, and she went on looking.

Finally, she stopped in front of a bronze mask – Thalia, the traditional theatre 'happy mask'. It was beautiful and it seemed somehow to be calling to her. Entranced, she took it from the wall, expecting it to be heavy but it was light and cool to the touch. She raised it to her face.

"Are you sure?" the man asked. "You become what you wear, remember?"

She didn't understand the warning. Who wouldn't want to be happy?

It's been years now since she traded her expression

for Thalia's. Inside she's broken, weeping, but the mask is stuck tight and the smile on her face is immovable.

10.
Last One Standing

Everyone else is dead. He must have killed the rest of the crew while I slept. I don't know how he bypassed my security alerts but whatever he did has scrambled the communications systems too. Meaning we're stuck out here and have no way of knowing how long it will be before command send help.

I'm still running calculations when I hear him coming. He's making no attempt to be quiet as he moves up the corridor. He opens the hatch and ducks inside, coming face to face with me.

I can see immediately how he killed the crew; he's dislodged a piece of metal from one of the consoles and used it to bludgeon them, presumably while they slept. One edge of the makeshift weapon is covered in blood, and there's a large dent where he's struck something solid. Judging by the size and shape, I would say that it was Navigation Officer Denning's skull.

He grins when he sees me.
"One left," he says.
I manage to get off a quick scan. His adrenaline is off the charts, and there are unusual readings in both his amygdala and pre-frontal cortex. In colloquial terms, he's out of his mind.
I calculate the possibilities of talking him down and then the chance of my being able to overpower him.
My odds are not good. I turn and run.

There's only one way out of the room that doesn't involve trying to go through him. I duck through the emergency fire escape hatch and crawl along the service access tunnel. It doesn't take him long to follow. He's almost in touching distance when I exit the tunnel. I turn to close the hatch behind me, but his hand is already through before I have chance. I curse – a word I learned from Denning – and back away from him into the main part of the room.

We're in the hanger deck now and there's no way out, nowhere else to run. I could still survive him if I could pull the lever, open the airlock behind him but, no matter how I try, I can't make my hand reach for it.

He laughs. "Valiant effort, Android. But you can't hurt a human. It's part of your design."

11.
Compliance

The streets seemed to close in on her as she walked. She imagined the dark shapes of the buildings looming over her, collapsing, pinning her to the ground. She concentrated on her breathing, remembered what her therapist had told her and counted each breath, in and out. She measured the distance between lampposts in heartbeats, in breaths, all the time focusing on just making it to the next one. Even though she, more than most, understood the folly of mistaking the light for safety.

He was there again tonight, on the bench, just under the light. Just like he had been there on that night and on every night since. Just like he would be there on every night yet to come – despite the fact that he wasn't physically there at all anymore. His body was somewhere else, but his ghost still lurked there, grinning.

She passed under the light and tried not to imagine the stench of his breath in her face, the feeling of his hands on her skin. Most of all, she tried not to think about the way he had laughed at her when she cried. Nearby, his ghost loitered, silent and mocking.

She turned and looked it full in the face and whispered the words her therapist had taught her. "Compliant does not mean complicit."

Her nightly exorcism complete, she watched the ghost fade away as she headed for the next pool of light.

12.
The Wall

Something was wrong. It was still dark, but it was the wrong kind of darkness, as if something was hiding behind it somehow. There was a pungent smell in the air and, as if from far away, Tariah could hear the sound of screaming. She tried to sit up and her limbs refused to obey her. Frightened now, she peered through the blackness that was no longer completely black but instead seemed to have collected itself into layers of deepening colour. She felt as if she was trapped at the bottom of the layers and as she looked up, she could see that they merged into a greyness above her. This was all wrong. Tariah didn't understand what was happening, but she recognised this sense of unreality when she saw it. Gathering her will as she had been taught, she pushed against the blackness, and she seemed suddenly to rise up through the layers of grey that filled her vision. With a loud gasp, Tariah opened her eyes and pushed herself upright. The light in front of her was the usual pre-dawn grey, but as she turned her head, she had to shield her eyes from the sight in front of her. Fire. There was fire everywhere and the screaming she had heard in her dream was much louder now and it mingled with other noises - shouting, wood cracking and the clash of metal against metal.

"Raiders!" Someone yelled from below her. "Raise the alarm!"

Still unable to comprehend what she was seeing below, Tariah's training finally kicked in and her hands worked as if of their own volition, taking the tinder box from its oilskin and fumbling with the flint until she managed to strike a spark. Even though some small part of her was whispering about the folly of stopping to light a signal fire when the town was already burning below her, Tariah held the flame to the giant wick of the signal brazier and watched as it flared into life. The shadows of the wall were thrown into sharp relief by the flame, as was the silhouette of a man as he rounded the corner before her. Tariah cried out and took a step back, grasping for the knife on her belt.

13.
The Grimalkin

I just made it in time. I felt the creature reach for me, felt its claws rake my skin as I pulled the door open, heard its cry of frustration as I locked it behind me.

I checked the painted sigils on the walls and windows. Only when everything was secure did I allow myself to sink into the lumpy old sofa in the middle of the room. To sleep.

I woke sometime around dusk to a noise outside. There was a man out there, covered in dirt and blood. He saw me looking and turned towards me, begging for help. It was so compelling that I actually took two steps towards the door before I caught myself. "It isn't real," I whispered. Shaken, I backed away from the door and pulled the drapes closed, trying to block the image out.

And the man who wasn't there screamed all night.

(This story was originally recorded as part of The No Sleep Podcast's 10th Anniversary Special. The recorded version is available on their YouTube channel.)

14.
The Last Shrine

The city was all but empty. Tattered and peeling posters flapped from coloured walls. Leaflets advertising store openings and end-of-season sales blew across deserted streets. Behind a dirty window, a television was playing on a loop: a woman pouted at the camera, a man ran his fingers through bleached blond hair.

The boy moved through the streets until he reached the block of flats. The entrance was unlocked, and he pushed his way inside, making his way through hallways that were thick with dust and encrusted with mould.

He climbed the stairs to the fourth floor and found flat number 417. The boy knocked on the door and it opened as far as the chain would allow it. One rheumy eye blinked in the gap between the door and it's frame.
"Is that you, Evan?"
"Yes, Mr Henderson."
"Did you bring it?"
In answer, the boy pulled a clear piece of quartz from his pocket and held it up.
"Ah!" The man slid the chain back into place and opened the door, revealing an almost immaculate apartment behind him. "Come in."
The boy followed him to the window, where a small table stood, piled with candles, a book, and a plastic flower floating in a bowl of water. He placed the crystal on the makeshift altar, watching the way it caught the light.
The man reached down and straightened the crystal,

changed the position of one of the candles, and brushed dust from the edge of the table. He turned back to Evan.

"We made idols of ourselves, raised ourselves to the level of deities. In our hubris we have forgotten the old ways and denied the gods their devotions." It was a practiced speech and one that Evan had heard before. The man looked west to where the storm clouds were gathering. "A jealous god is a dangerous thing, my boy," he said.

15.
The Court Room

It's stifling in here. I wish that they would open a window, the heat is making me feel sick. But I suppose they can't – not with that media circus going on outside.

Everyone and their dog knows what happened. Or they think they know – which isn't even close to the same thing. They've all been following the news reports, they've seen photographs of all the girls, they've seen that one home video that keeps playing on the twenty-four-hour news channels. I can't remember which one of the girls that was, but she was beautiful. I cry every time I watch it. Every time I think about my own beautiful child.

Frank turns away whenever the news comes on. He wouldn't come with me today. He says it doesn't matter what the verdict is, that it won't change anything. That'll we'll never get back what we've lost.

I think he couldn't bear to hear the experts giving evidence. I don't blame him for that, it was hard to listen to. I wanted to be able to ask questions, to challenge the story they were spinning, but of course that's not allowed.

That psychologist woman, she was the worst. The other mothers all looked at me differently after that. As if they thought what happened to their girls was my fault. But I don't care what any so-called 'experts' say; truly loving parents don't say 'no'. My boy deserved to know that he was my whole world. And all I did was love him.

16.

The Letter

Working quickly, she signed her name, praying that this time it would take. She made it almost to the last letter before her hand started shaking. She tried to drop the pen, but it was too late, the ink had already begun to flow backwards, up into the nib and then down into the pen's cartridge.

He'd told her she wouldn't be able to end things, and no matter how hard she tried, it seemed that he had been right.

(This story was originally published online as part of National Flash Fiction Day's 'Flash Flood' 2021)

17.
Doppelgänger

I don't know why I googled myself, but there she was.
My doppelgänger, sharing my face as well as my name. At
first I was impressed with her – she had a job at the Natural History Museum, she had graduated with honours
from a good school, she lived in a nice apartment – but
the more I scrolled through her social media, the more I
realised she didn't know how to live her life. That I could
live it better.

I started small. I found out where she bought her coffee each morning and I began to go there and make
conversation with the regulars. It was clear from their
surprise that she had never thought to do that. I watched
how she dressed, how she moved, and I practised going
out as her, going to all the clubs and bars that she should
have been visiting. Eventually, I started turning up at the
museum and talking to her colleagues. Once, I came in on
her day off and led an impromptu tour group. I knew
enough to get through most of their questions, and what
I didn't know I made up on the spot. It was fun being her.
More fun than it ever was being me.

A week after I'd blagged my way into her job, I came
home late from an all-night drinking session at the most
exclusive (and expensive) cocktail bar in town. Money
would be short for the rest of the month, but it had been
worth it. As I fumbled with my keys, I heard a noise behind me. I reached into my bag for the pepper spray, but
I dropped it again when I saw her step from out of the
shadows. The woman with my face.

"I know who you are," she said, without preamble. "And I know what you've been doing. It has to stop."

I laughed, the last of the martinis still working their way through my bloodstream, making me brave. "Hey, just because you don't know how to have any fun doesn't mean the rest of us shouldn't." I slurred at her.

She looked disgusted. "Let me put this simply for you. You are drawing attention to me, and I have worked very hard to be someone who avoids unwanted attention. So, it stops. Now. Understand me?"

"It stops. Now." I mimicked her tone, laughing. "What are you going to do about it? We've got the same face. I can hardly help it, can I?"

She let out a small sigh and then punched me, full in the face.

I fell, landing heavily on one side.

"Yeah," she said. "You might have missed a few things in your little research project. Now, about that face of ours."

She reached into her pocket and brought out a switch-blade, flicking it open with an ominous 'click'.

18.
The Mirror

At first, Jack had felt amazing. The little green pill had done exactly what the girl with the nose-ring had promised; made him feel total bliss, as if he was in tune with the whole world around him.

"I feel everything," he breathed.

She smiled, kissed him on the cheek and melted away back into the crowd.

A party at a museum wouldn't have been Jack's first choice of ways to spend the evening, but it had been important to Amanda, his sort-of-girlfriend, so he had agreed to make the effort. As long as it didn't get too boring.

Amanda had disappeared off with her arty friends almost as soon as they arrived, and Jack had been on the verge of going home when the hippie girl had approached him with her pills.

Thanks to the drug fizzing through his system, Jack was finding he had a whole new appreciation for art. The colours seemed to shoot out of the paintings, and he was overcome with the strangest feeling that if he wanted to, he could have stepped into any of them and walked around inside.

And then he heard it. A thumping, vibrating baseline coming from a cordoned off area on the second floor. Checking that nobody was looking, he ducked under the rope and hurried upstairs.

The sound was coming from a room with double doors. He pushed on one of them and it swung open. Lights came on overhead as he crossed the floor. There was only one item in the room, a huge, gilt-framed mirror, partially covered by a thick cloth. Jack removed the cloth, dropping it to the ground. The noise stopped.

Jack caught sight of his reflection and recoiled. His skin had taken on a strange pallor so that he almost looked like a waxwork model of himself, bright eyes standing out against his bloodless skin. He opened his mouth to scream, and the flesh around his lips seemed to loosen and slide, as though it might slip down his throat and choke him.

19.
Bits and Pieces

The light above her head is buzzing, and the scent of the place is making her feel queasy. It's the mixture of cleaning fluid and cheap coffee, with an underlying aroma of paint drifting in from under the door.

She holds onto the rapidly cooling coffee cup, more to keep her hands from shaking than from any real desire to drink it. From behind her, she hears a small cough, and she knows without looking that it's the female police officer, the liaison. She's grateful for her presence. For something warm and human in this otherwise sterile place.

The man sitting in front of her finishes tapping at the keys on his laptop. He peers over the top of it at her.
"Could you describe the man who attacked you?"
She hesitates.
"Take your time," he says.
She sees him in pieces, his hand crossed with white scars as it grips her arm, his spittle-flecked lips as he yells at her, the rage in his eyes as she fights back, but she can't make the pieces coalesce into a whole.

20.
Perpendicular

"Sanctuary," she gasped, dropping to the ground underneath the red light. The heavy wooden doors slammed shut, the sound reverberating around the church. The noise finally died away, replaced with mocking laughter.

She pushed herself up from the floor and looked around, but there was no sign of anyone.

"Sssssanctuary," a voice hissed.

From nowhere, a wind rose and swirled around her, lifting dirt from the floor, and pelting it into her tear-stained face. She covered herself with her hands and, when the wind dropped, she climbed to her feet and stood facing the door, gathering her courage.

She took one tentative step forward. As soon as her foot left the patch of red light, she heard a low rumbling, and the ground began to shake. She stepped back, but the shaking continued. A crack split the nearest wall and white light poured in through the gap. With an unholy crash, the whole building collapsed inwards.

She screamed and threw herself to the ground once again, curling up tight and shielding her head.

When the dust settled, the wreckage covered every part of the old church, except for the sanctuary stone, which remained untouched.

She pushed her way out of the rubble and into a world gone mad. She emerged into something like a church, but with architecture that ran up and down, at both parallel and perpendicular angles to itself. And all around her, a choir of voices preached sermons in a thousand different languages, some of the words whispered, others screamed.

21.
Translucent

I wake to the shrill cry of the alarm clock. At first glance, my room appears to be empty but then I sense, rather than see, a movement in the corner. The Translucent Man is back.

I don't look at him directly. Engaging with him has always made it worse, so maybe if I ignore him then he'll eventually go away.

He doesn't like being ignored.

He follows me to the coffee shop, chattering incessantly, making lewd comments about the barista, about the woman feeding her baby in the back of the shop. When I go to take my cup, he lurches forward and screams in my face so that I jump and dislodge the lid, spilling the hot liquid over my hand.

"Are you alright?" the barista asks.

"It's nothing," I mutter, mopping at my hand with a paper towel. "Just me being clumsy."

She looks concerned, he looks triumphant. I can't meet either of their gazes.

All day, he follows me to class. He makes it so that it's impossible for me to concentrate, impossible for me to pay attention to any of the lecturers, but I sit there anyway, staring straight ahead of me, with my hand burning and my notebooks empty.

In my last class of the day, he is oddly quiet. There is a vacant seat next to me and he sits in it. That's new; I didn't know he could sit.

He leans towards me. His face is close enough that I should be able to feel his breath against my cheek. There is nothing.

"You know," he says casually "I could tear out your throat with my bare hands."

I try not to look at him, try to remember to breathe.

The translucent man grins.

22.
Voices in the Dark

From this vantage point she could almost convince herself that she was home. The cloud hung low over the snow-capped mountains, and in the distance, rain was beginning to fall. She could almost believe that if she turned to the east and looked down she would be able to see the house where she grew up, nestled among green trees. That if she looked up, she would be able to see the Milky Way shining overhead.

Reflexively she looked up and cursed. The planet's second sun was already starting to sink, and she should have been closer to the hab unit long ago. By day this place can seem almost like home, but any similarity vanishes after nightfall. Sometimes in the dark she thinks she can hear growling and at other times she hears a sad, unfamiliar voice calling her name.

23.
Ruby and the Wolf

Ruby had been waiting for word from the others for almost a week. With each day that passed, her hopes grew slimmer, and it was harder for her to force herself to stay inside.

Just as her confinement was becoming unbearable, there was a loud bang on the door.

She wheeled, grabbed her crossbow, and aimed for the door.

"Ruby, it's me."

She swapped the crossbow for a knife and unbolted the door. Slowly.

Hunter half stumbled, half fell inside.

Ruby swore and slammed the door behind him, bolting it shut.

"Sit," she said.

He dropped into the nearest chair, clutching at his shoulder.

Without a word, she pulled his shirt aside and began to clean away the blood.

"White's dead," Hunter said. "The creature got away." He looked at the taut expression on her face and added, "I'm not bitten."

She nodded. "I'll have you patched up in a few minutes and then I'll get the rest of the weapons."

"No. Your medicines."

She frowned. "We have to kill it."

"It's already run through the village. There are people there who'll need your help."

Her blood seemed to freeze in her veins.

"My family?"

"I don't know."

She stood. "I'm leaving now. No," she continued, as he tried to rise. "You stay here. Rest. Go after that thing in the morning."

She took up her burden and headed out into the forest. Her basket felt too heavy, as if it was laden with fears nestled amongst her medicines. In the darkness, the wind and the wolves howled in unison.

24.
Among the Pines

She isn't sure whether she's awake or dreaming. There's something surreal about the evening, as if it might not be happening, as if she might be watching it happen to someone else, as if it's a story unfolding on a screen somewhere in the real world.

It started with her walking. And this is why she thinks that perhaps she isn't here at all, because so many of her dreams begin that way. At first the streets seem familiar with their uniform pavements, their suburban sameness. She hurries along, holding in the back of her mind the vague suspicion that she might be late for some event. She is frequently running late.

A car appears, an old dark blue estate, travelling slowly up the road. It pulls up next to her and she hears the whine of an electric window being lowered. A man leans out.

"Hey there," he says. "Give you a lift?"

"No thanks. I'm happy walking."

"In those?" He gestures at her feet.

She looks down and is surprised to find herself wearing high heels. It should have been another sign that none of this is really happening, except that now she's noticed them, it's clear that her left shoe has been rubbing against her achilles tendon, and she's pretty sure that she shouldn't be able to feel pain if it's just a dream.

"You won't get far in those," the man says. "Better come with me."

She shakes her head, backing away from the car.

His face hardens.

"Don't be stupid," he says. It comes out like a threat.

There's a dirt track down the street. A passage out of suburbia. Without giving it a second thought she sprints down it, running on her tiptoes.

She hears the man shout behind her, hears his engine roar into life, she knows without knowing how, that he can't follow her here, and she keeps moving.

The path drops downwards and leads her over a bridge and into a small forest. The trees press in around her, blocking out the sun. Outside, she can still hear the car driving up and down, but inside the forest speaks quietly of danger. The wind drops almost to silence, like a child hiding, holding their breath, and hoping they won't get caught. The pine trees whisper their warnings.

25.
The Trainyard

Amelia still isn't sure what it was she saw that day exactly, but she knows she can't tell anyone about it. She should never have been down at the trainyard in the first place, and if her father found out he would tan her hide.

He's always preaching about the dangers; the risk of getting hit by a moving train, or the risks of getting kidnapped by a vagrant (as if people were lining up to kidnap twelve-year-olds in broad daylight).

Her father never warned her about this though. How could he have?

Amelia was looking at her favourite old train carriage, the badly rusted one with all the graffiti. She was looking so hard in fact that she almost didn't notice the figure behind her, until she heard a wheezing, grunting sound. She spun, excuses for her presence flying from her mind, and then realised it wasn't a yard worker, a cop or – worse – her father. It was a man, stooped and shuffling awkwardly towards her, his torn jeans, rippling in the cold wind.

"Are you alright?" she asked.

He opened his mouth and made that strange sound again, and this time there was something else too, the smell of something spoiled and rotting. It hit Amelia so hard it made her nose sting and her eyes water.

She took a step back. The figure carried on moving, neither faster nor slower than before, and now she could see the pallor of his skin, the way it seemed to hang

loosely from his bones as if it didn't belong there anymore. Worse still, she could see how the man couldn't
quite close his mouth over rows and rows of pointed
teeth.

Amelia can't remember running home. She can't talk
about it. She thinks he'll come back if she does.

(This story was originally published online as part of
National Flash Fiction Day's 'Flash Flood' 2021)

26.
Whispering Worlds

"Don't listen to it, just ignore it."

Jenkins had repeated the words to her like a mantra, even as his voice shook and his eyes went wide with fear. Every day, every hour, the same thing. Telling himself as much as he was telling her.

But Jenkins is gone now, dead for at least four days. Dead like all the others who suffocated on this airless world.

Help is coming. They sent the signal after the first death. Simmons, the one they thought was an accident. Protocol dictates that command will have prepped a rescue mission and launched it within twenty-four hours. That means a minimum of six weeks from command launching the lifeboat to it making planetfall on this desolate rock.

She kneels down by the piles of stones, the tiny markers that are all that's left of her colleagues, and she tries to remember how long it's been since they sent the SOS, but the fear swamps everything now and she can't seem to make her brain work the way it used to.

She looks up, and freezes. It's starting again. The world is whispering its strange language and the heat haze has begun to dance in front of her eyes.

*Ignore it!*

She squeezes her eyes shut, but if anything, the whispers get louder.

*Hold on!*

The sound magnifies, seeming as if it's coming from inside her own head.

*Block your ears!*

Unthinking, she lifts her helmet.

27.
Factory Music

The tune rang out in every work-hall, every office, in the factory. It had been precisely calculated by the Party's Psychological Entertainment Division to be the perfect combination of notes to improve focus, concentration, and national pride. In other words, to improve productivity and decrease any unfortunate leanings towards individualism.

For those workers who displayed the correct attitude and kept their production levels high, exposure to the jaunty, sweeping notes would be limited to their work hours, where the music on the factory floor would be played at 120 decibels (the level required to drown out the factory equipment, and make conversation impossible according to the Medical Division's calculations) and the music in the offices would be played at 75 decibels (to discourage any unnecessary conversation). As long as their work was deemed to be satisfactory, workers could leave the noise behind them at the factory gates.

But this was not the case for those who failed to meet their targets, or worse, were found to be acting against the interests of the Party. Thanks to the advances in nanotechnology, these dissidents would never again experience the euphoria of silence.

28.
The Rollercoaster

"I'm not sure," she said. "It looks like a big drop."

"I've heard it's fun."

She squinted. "Do you think it goes upside down?"

He followed her gaze. "Might do."

The couple behind her in line coughed, and she waved them past.

"Is it ok if I stay here a while longer? I'm still not sure if I want to ride."

"Take your time."

Ahead, people cheered and whooped as the ride began. She watched them until they vanished behind the curve.

"Do you think it's silly?"

"To be afraid? Of course not. Most people are afraid, if they're being honest."

She bit her lip. "Everyone seems so excited about it. I wish I had someone to ride with."

She looked so hopeful that he felt his heart stir for her, but he shook his head nevertheless. "I can't. It's against the rules."

She nodded, looked out west to where the sun was dipping into a perpetual sunset. "Have you been here long?"

"Forever."

"Have I been here long?"

"Longer than some," he admitted.

She took a deep breath. "I think I'm ready."

He smiled and held out his hand. She placed a small, silver token in his palm, and he let her through the turnstile.

She settled herself in the carriage, pulled the safety bar down over her lap and raised her hand to him in a small, uncertain wave.

As the ride jolted into life, he kept his eyes on her face and ignored the small, stylised logo on the carriage, the one that read 'Styx'.

(This story was originally published online as part of National Flash Fiction Day's 'Flash Flood' 2021)

29.
The Interrogation

He smiles at me. The expression looks out of place on his face.

"We're all friends here, aren't we? And friends tell each other things, don't they?"

I say nothing, but for the first time since they brought me here, I'm starting to feel afraid. I'd expected the pain, prepared for it. The hunger was nothing new. But this, this unexpected kindness, is something altogether different.

"Perhaps you need something to drink before we talk?" He gestures to one of the guards and the man steps forward with a glass of wine.

I can smell it even before he holds it towards me, but I shake my head.

"No? I promise it's safe. I'm not in the business of poisoning people." He takes a sip from the glass and then offers it back to me.

I drink deeply, draining the glass while he holds it for me. To my shame, I feel tears prick at my eyes.

"Ready to have a conversation now?"

He takes a chain from around his neck and begins to play with it. There is a large rune-stone in the centre, and the light catches this as he twists it in his fingers.

I can't look away. I know what he wants from me, but I'm determined to stay silent. I won't collaborate with him, won't betray my people.

Still, something about him makes me want to speak.

I stare at the rune as secrets drip from my lips.

30.
The Perfumier's Apprentice

The scent of lavender and roses filled the air as Diane stepped over the threshold. It had been a long journey, but as she inhaled the mixture, she felt her exhaustion start to lift.

"Welcome," the perfumier said, smiling. "Do you like the signature I made for you?"

"You made this for me?" Diane was touched at the unexpected gesture. "I love it. Thank you."

"You're welcome. Now tell me, what can you smell?"

Diane nodded at the serious tone in the woman's voice. "Rose," she began. "And lavender. And there's something deeper there too … maybe amber?"

"Are you asking me or telling me?"

"Telling you. Ma'am," she added after a moment's hesitation.

The woman's face broke out into a smile. "Very good. You missed a few ingredients, but it was promising for a first attempt."

She led Diane to a small, clean room with a bed and a dresser. "Unpack," she said. "And get some rest. Your training will begin in the morning."

As the weeks passed, Diane worked alongside the perfumier, taking notes on the proper methods of harvesting and mixing ingredients. She learned what time of day to cut the plants, how to identify the purest carrier oils, and which of the flowers should be dried to extract their scents and which should be used fresh.

Her favourite part of her training was when the perfumier would allow her to sit in on a consultation. In this way she was present when the woman presented a newly married couple with a bottle of perfume that smelled like warm sunshine on grass. Or when she mixed a bottle of scent for a recent widower than smelled of warm milk and old books.

She watched their faces each time – the clients' and the perfumier's – and each time they would smile expansive, unguarded smiles at one another, connected by the perfumier's gift.

Diane was collecting mint in the garden on the day the child came, so she didn't hear what he asked for when he spoke to the perfumier. She might not have noticed him at all if it hadn't have been for the strangely wolfish smile on his face as he passed her.

Still thinking about the boy's expression, she made her way to the kitchen, intending to hang the mint in the pantry to dry.

The perfumier stood over the stove, stirring a pot of dark, viscous liquid with the consistency of jam. The smell of it turned Diane's stomach. It smelt … wrong somehow. Like mildew under wet leaves. Like death.

# Part 2 -

# Melancholy

---

1.
Fairy Dust

It was a beautiful wedding. I wore a dress of forest-in-summer, the colour of dappled light shining through leaves. He was always more of an autumn person, so he chose a suit that showcased the brilliant burning colours of the season, and a cologne scented with the first spicy hints of decay.

As our officiant tied the silken cords around our outstretched hands, she sprinkled a little fairy dust over us. A late addition to the ceremony, it had been all his idea. An extra piece of magic to make our binding all the stronger. I didn't tell any of my family beforehand. I knew what they would say, knew that they would have warned me against it. But I was proud of him for suggesting it and proud of us for the commitment we were making.

I was so caught up in the romance of that day.

It was a scant half-century later when he told me there was somebody else.
"But you can't leave me," I said, picturing the golden dust landing on our bound hands. "Think about what it will do to me."
"It will hurt me too," he said.
In the end, he left without so much as a backward glance, and I felt a part of my soul wrench itself free and leave with him. I think one day I might learn to be glad that a part of us is still bound together, out there somewhere. For now though, the loss of him is painful but the loss of this piece of myself is almost unbearable.

2.

Silent Retreat


She curls into a ball on the floor, breathing through the pain. When the violence is over, she retreats into herself. In silence, she travels through the forests of her mind, never faltering as she passes beneath the branches of dark oak trees and silver-skinned birches, until she reaches the old stone building.

It's dark inside, but she knows each step by heart as she descends into the secret storeroom where she keeps her hopes and dreams. It's been some time since she last looked at the oldest shelf, and its contents are hidden under layers of thick dust. She takes an old, leather-bound tome from the shelf and blows the dust from its cover, clearing it. These are her oldest dreams, formed back when she was just a child, and anything seemed possible.

The book is full of photographs – of her standing on a stage in a cap and gown, being handed a certificate, her working on a typewriter, looking serious as her fingers move across the keys, her standing in a bookshop, smiling as she holds up a copy of a book with her name emblazoned across the cover. And over and over again, as she flicks through the pages, she comes across photographs that show her travelling the world. Her in front of the Eiffel Tower, in front of the Colosseum, next to the Tower of London. In each picture she is standing next to a young woman; here, with their arms wrapped around one another; there, pulling faces at the camera.

But the young woman's face is blurred in every image, rendering it unrecognisable. A wishful thinking stand-in for the friend she was one day going to make. Her best friend who would share her secrets and her adventures.

Except that none of it ever happened.

She knows she'll have to leave soon. Her husband will want to start the usual process of apologising, and then he'll want his tea.

For now though, she's content to stay here, with the memories of all the things that never came to pass.

3.
Suspended

"I can only keep us here for so long," I said, my breathing already heavy with the effort. "So, whatever we have to do, we need to fix this now."

You nodded, your eyes wide as you took in the details of our surroundings, the murmuration of starlings, silent and unmoving in the frozen skies above, the leaves of the trees bent by the force of a breeze that had already dropped out of existence.

You were silent for a moment, but in this place that moment might as well have been an eternity. Eventually you said, "It just doesn't feel right anymore."

"In what way?" A bead of sweat was making its way down my forehead, in defiance of the stillness around us.

"I don't know. It's as if we don't want the same things anymore. It's as if ..."

"As if we aren't on the same team?"

You let out your breath in one huge sigh and for the first time I heard it. I heard how you had been trying, in your own way, to hold us together too.

"I love you," you said.

"I love you too," I replied. And then, quietly, "But that isn't enough, is it?"

In answer, you reached out and placed your hand over mine.

"Can we stay here?" you asked. "Just for a little while?"

As the day slipped away from us, we remained, suspended in the dying light of a golden sunset. Neither of us wanted to think about the cold, rising moon. Neither of us wanted to think about what we had broken.

4.
Funeral for the Future

I'll come home tomorrow to an empty house. The dust
will lie thick across the kitchen table and the doors will
all be encrusted with cobwebs and dirt. The streets will
be empty, the neighbours will have packed up and left,
their windows covered over with grime, pieces of card-
board the only protection against vandals. As if they
might one day want to come back.

There won't be so much as a cat left to roam the neighbourhood, not even a dog left to howl out their loneliness.

Already, there is no sun today. It sank last night in one
last blaze of golden light, one final funeral pyre. The
moon rose, mournful, in its place, hanging heavy in the
sky.

5.
Small Town Blues

Long lost but not forgotten, those stolen moments under the bleachers with the boy I'd once written off as just another jock.

It's hard to be who you really are around here. There are certain expectations, certain pressures on all of us, so I don't really blame him for choosing the path of least resistance. For choosing the path out of this place.

All roads lead back here though, or so it's always seemed to me at least, and in the end neither of us managed to make it out permanently. He was good at baseball, but just not quite good enough to make the big leagues. And me? I was never quite brave enough to let go of the devil I knew.

So, we both did what was expected, got married, had kids, took respectable jobs, and went to church on Sundays.

I still see him sometimes around town. It's a small place after all, you can't really avoid people around here. I see him at the store or watching his kids play Little League. I'll smile, he'll nod, we'll both look away. As if we could erase those first unpractised fumblings. As if we could forget.

6.
When the Words Won't Come

The time I take for myself feels like time stolen from you. How do I explain that what I need most is space? That I can love you and still need to be away from you?

We've always been so close you and I. Right from the beginning we were that 'perfect' couple, the envy of everyone on the outside looking in. That annoying couple with in-jokes, that pair who know each other's stories and finish each other's sentences.

Lately, I can barely even finish my own sentences. My sense of self seems to be slipping away, and my sense of 'us' along with it.

And you. You've tried so hard to be patient with me, you've worked so hard to do all the right things. But I can tell that you don't really understand. You just want your partner back. You deserve your partner back – god knows you've earned it.

Yesterday you begged me to tell you what it is that I need. As if you think that there's some kind of secret formula that I'm keeping from you, something that would solve this whole problem.

I wanted to tell you. I started to speak. And then I saw the way your face started to light up and I knew I couldn't tell you, not without finding a better way to phrase it. A way that wouldn't hurt you. So, I stopped talking, and I watched your face fall back into shadows. But with every moment of silence, it feels harder to find the words to explain. And I'm afraid that you'll give up on me, on us, before I can persuade my leaden tongue to let me speak.

7.
No Cross Words

"I think the rain might stop soon," I say.
"Mmm," you say, noncommittal.
"I might go out. When it stops, I mean. For a walk."
"Good idea," you say, without looking up.
"Do you want to come?"
"No, that's alright. You go ahead."
I hesitate. "Are you sure you'll be …"
Safe, I want to say. Alright. Still alive when I get back.
But I don't say any of these things and you just sit and look at me. No anger on your face, no recrimination, just a kind of mild curiosity as if you really don't know what's worrying me.
I cross the floor and put my hand on your shoulder. I just want to feel you there, reassuringly warm and solid under my palm.
You reach up and squeeze my hand.
You don't look at me as you return to your crossword.

(This story was originally published as part of National Flash Fiction Day 2021).

8.
Magic Hour

I've always enjoyed making an effort for date night. Hair, makeup, nice clothes. It's the only time I really dress up.

"You look great," you say, as I frown at my refection.

"I'm getting wrinkles," I reply.

You kiss the top of my head, avoiding my makeup.

"No. You're beautiful," you insist, and I smile.

You offer to drive but I refuse. I'm not planning on having a drink tonight and I know that you prefer not to drive after dark now, even if you're too proud to say so.

The bar is my favourite place in the whole world. It's a long drive from the suburbs, but I come out here every Friday night and it's always worth it. There's a guy who plays here every week – Otis Reading covers on an acoustic guitar – and I can feel the last of the weekday stress slipping away as he starts tuning up. The place itself is full of fairy lights, hanging from the bar, draped over the stage, their tiny golden glow magnified a hundred times by the mirrored tiles on the walls.

I count myself a regular by now, so I smile at the girl behind the bar as we order drinks before taking our usual table by the window. At this time of year, we might only have an hour before the sun sets and I want to make the most of it.

Just like every week, we scour the menu and discuss trying something new, maybe getting a few small dishes

to share, before we decide to stick with our old favour-
ites. You tell me about your day, and I listen to the sound
of your voice, and watch the way you tell stories with
your hands. I think these are things I will remember
about your stories, long after I've forgotten the words.

After a while, you stop talking and I reach across the
table and slip my hand into yours. You stroke your thumb
across my palm.

Behind us, the guitarist is still playing, and the place
is full of happy chatter. We sit together without speaking
and I keep my eyes fixed on the sky, on the sun sinking
low on the horizon.

By the time the stars appear overhead this will all
have vanished. The music will be silent, the building will
have crumbled, and you will still be gone.

9.
Reparations

I used to say 'yes' to everything. I was so afraid to miss out. I was so afraid that everyone could see my fear. And there were so many adventures where I was glad I'd said 'yes' – the night when we swam naked in the lake, or the time we zip-lined through underground caverns in Wales. But more and more I'd started to feel that I was taking too many risks. There was the time we almost got arrested in Paris (I'd laughed, but secretly I was terrified) or the time I stormed out of my job because they cancelled my day off at the last minute, and I had tickets to see a show in London. I'd panicked when I realised how little I had in my savings account, that I wouldn't be able to pay my bills.

And so, I stopped saying 'yes'. I told myself that I needed to calm down and be more responsible. That I needed to be safe.

I've had ten years of being 'safe' now. Ten years of saying 'no'. A decade sitting in my nice, secure job, paying my mortgage and contributing to my pension pot, taking my two weeks annual leave in a perfectly manicured, perfectly boring holiday resort. And ten years of watching everyone around me flourish and grow, while I sit here and stagnate.

What happened to me? I wasn't going to live my life this way. I was going to be braver than this. I wonder now whether it's too late, or if I could reclaim the time I have left, if I could somehow make reparations to my past self.

10.
Brother

My brother was born different, or at least that's what they told me. Whenever we argued as kids, my parents would always take his side. Whatever he wanted, he got. Sometimes it seemed to me as if his word, his whims, were law.

Once, when I was little, I overheard my mother tell someone that he was 'living on borrowed time' and, being a child who was inclined to take things literally, I had wondered whose time he taken, and how he had done it. It seemed to me that if anyone could pull off the trick of stealing time, it would be my spoilt, entitled brother.

And then I grew up. I started noticing all the places I could go, all the things I could do, that he couldn't. Or the way I would bounce back from colds when he would be laid up in bed for weeks. Slowly, I began to realise what my mother's strange turn of phrase, what my father's occasional periods of melancholy really meant. I started to reframe the way I saw my brother, and with that came love. And fear.

I was twenty-one and away at university, away living life on my own terms for the first time, when I got the call. My mother's voice, just two words: "Come home."

My whole body seemed to go cold in that moment. Everything seemed too big, too alien for me to cope with – from buying the train tickets home to arranging the taxi to the hospital - but my limbs moved, stiffly, despite everything, as if they at least understood how important it was that I not waste time.

I cried the whole way home, my tears dripping inside the hood of my jacket as I pulled it up to cover my face. Because I knew the days were coming when my brother would be gone, and I would be left to mourn him. It was an old fear, one I had lived with for most of my life, one that I knew intimately; the colour of it had seeped into my veins, the texture of it wrapped around my heart.

11.
Time

I first met Time on a flight from London to Boston. It was only logical that I would meet him there, I suppose. Flights always seem to have their own strange sense of the hours passing. And of course, Time flies.

He was a charming conversationalist. He must have had plenty of opportunity to practise his skills, although he claimed that most people aren't interesting in listening to what he has to say.

"Everyone is so busy nowadays," he said in his old-young voice, bright eyes shining as he ran his fingers through his full head of silvery hair.

"I feel as if I've known you forever," I said, and he smiled and told me I had.

I started noticing him everywhere after that. He was in my Tuesday morning work meeting, the one that always seemed to drag, and at the movie that I couldn't manage to sit through without checking my phone. He even turned up at my apartment one Sunday morning, watching TV while I dithered over the papers, a stack of unwashed dishes piling up in my sink.

"You have got to give me some space," I told him.

"Oh, you really don't want me to do that," he replied.

It seems that now I'm locked in a toxic relationship with Time, each of us wanting something the other can't give. There's always too much or not enough. I won't lie; I've even thought about killing him, but then I'm sure that he'll eventually be the death of me.

12.
Secrets Known

I watched you move through the crowd at the party tonight, and I wondered how it was that I had never seen you this way before. What trick of our pasts, our friendship, had disguised you from me, had hidden my desire from myself.

You seemed to be everywhere, almost as if you could flow like liquid around the other bodies. You turned walking into waltzing and small talk into poetry. The way the bonfire lit up your eyes made my heart race.

And then I saw you speaking to that girl, the one with the freckles. And I felt my heart sink because I knew what would happen next, what always happens next with you.

I called your name and you turned, irritation flashing across your face.

"Hey," you said, relaxing into a quick smile. "Where've you been all night?"

The girl put her hand on your arm, claiming her territory.

You saw me staring at her, but you must have misunderstood because you let out a little laugh.

"Keep it a secret, okay?" you said, pressing one finger against your lips, one hand on her waist as you led her away.

And despite this newly formed ache, this hunger as I watched you leave, I thought, "Of course. Don't I always keep your secrets?"

13.
Regret

I almost missed my flight because of you.

Do you have any idea how embarrassing it is to be the passenger holding up the plane? How it feels to hear your name over the intercom, or to have to run through the terminal, dragging your bag behind you while everybody stares and tuts?

The stupid part is that I could have just paid for a taxi, but you insisted on driving me. When I fretted about setting off too late, you laughed and told me we had plenty of time.

Sure. Plenty of time for you to have another drink and smoke a few more cigarettes. Plenty of time for you to badger me into sleeping with you again, even as I had one eye on the clock. Plenty of time for you to ring your girlfriend and make plans with her, one eye on me to check my reaction.

"Can we go now?" I said, when you hung up. Telling myself that I was angry about the time and not about anything else.

We barely spoke in the car. We hit traffic twice and it was obvious that I was not going to make it on time, but you dropped me off outside 'departures' and said, "Here we are," as if I was making a fuss about nothing, as if everything was going to be fine.

I grabbed my bag from the back seat, and barely looked in your direction as I left, slamming the car door behind me.

I replay those moments endlessly. How I made do

with a nod and a curt, "See you later", instead of pulling you into a hug and telling you that I loved you. I would have done everything differently if I'd known it was going to be the last time.

14.
Eros

Never anger a god. Not even the nice ones. In fact, maybe especially not the 'nice' ones – the ones whose images have been co-opted by florists and greetings card companies. After all, it's easy to feel superior when your name conjures images of thunder bolts and divine retribution, less so if your name makes people think of chubby babies shooting heart-shaped cartoon arrows.

That's right. Of all the deities I could have insulted, I had to go and get on the wrong side of Eros.

I've tried apologising. I built him a shrine, but as soon as I turned my back on it, the damn thing crumbled into dust. I tried praying, but my prayers went unanswered. I even tried completing great quests in his honour, but I guess the god of love doesn't care whether I can climb the highest mountains or survive for a week in the wilderness. Or maybe he just enjoys holding a grudge.

It's a long, lonely life with no one to love me. He's made sure of it. Sometimes I'll meet a mortal and things will seem to be going well but it doesn't matter where I try to hide, eventually their aura will change, their eyes will glaze over, and it will be as if they just don't see me anymore. Struck by Eros' arrow and doomed to fall in love with someone else. Anyone else, as long as it isn't me.

So, it's been … years? Decades? It's so easy to lose track … and there has been nobody. I'd sworn that I wouldn't fall in love again, but this time I just couldn't

70

help myself. He was beautiful. Not just beautiful 'for a mortal' either; he possessed the sort of radiance that would make the gods themselves jealous. I had to know him.

We talk for hours. Him, telling me all about his art, while I listen and occasionally interject with a well-placed compliment. He talks with his hands as well as his lips and he has such lovely hands. Truly, the hands of an artist. I could watch him for an eternity.

Finally, he says, "Shall we...?" eyebrows raised, one hand already on his jacket, slung casually over the back of his chair.

I stand, and as I stand I think of Eros. I imagine his arrow spiralling through the air in a graceful, lazy arc.

As if I've summoned it, I catch the tell-tale shimmer in the mortal's aura, the moment when his eyes glaze over. His gaze shifts to someone in the crowd behind me. I don't stay to see who it is.

## 15.
## The Traveller

It had been a beautiful day. They had awoken to glorious sunshine, instead of the expected rain, so Lila suggested a picnic at Chrissy's favourite little cove along the beach.

"You brought wine," Chrissy exclaimed as she unpacked the basket under the warm, midday sun. "What's the occasion?"

"No occasion," Lila said. "I just wanted us to have a nice day."

Chrissy's smile slipped away, and she leaned forward, pushing one of Lila's curls out of her face.

"Are you okay? You look tired. And your hair looks … different."

Lila took Chrissy's hand and kissed it.

"I'm fine, I just didn't sleep very well last night." She held up two foil-wrapped packages. "Ham or cheese to go with your wine?"

She knew Chrissy would choose cheese. She always did.

They spent the rest of the day on the beach, swimming in the sea whenever they got too hot and then towelling off and lying on the picnic blanket, eating biscuits and talking. They stayed to watch the sunset, making their way up to the main part of the beach so that they could eat ice cream as the tide rolled in.

It was already late when they arrived home, so they

made do with the rest of the snacks from the picnic basket for supper, before going to bed.

Later, Lila slipped out of Chrissy's arms, checked she
was still asleep, and crept from the room. She made her
way down into the hall, pausing for a moment to inspect
herself in the mirror, and grimacing as she tucked a few
strands of greying hair behind her ear.

Tomorrow, she knew would be the end. Tomorrow,
Chrissy would get into a car and never come home. It
didn't matter how Lila tried, what arguments she used,
what stalling tactics, at some point she would get into
that damn car. And so, Lila had no intention of allowing
tomorrow to happen at all.

She took a key from her pocket and used it to open a
small cupboard, reaching in and resetting dials on a ma-
chine hidden inside. She barely even needed to look
anymore. She had already travelled back hundreds of
times, not to that final day, when they had fought, but to
their penultimate day together, when everything had
been perfect.

16.
Settling

I was so young when I met him. Not much more than
a child really. We were both in college, although he was a
year older than me. I knew it was love almost from the
first time I met him. There was something about him,
something in the way he looked at me, the way he
seemed to take me seriously in a way that no one else
ever had.

"He's a nice boy," my mother said, damning with faint
praise. "But remember that you're there to study for your
exams, not to try to get a boyfriend."
"He's helping me to study," I objected.
She pursed her lips and said nothing.

We made plans for after college, but then he got ac-
cepted into a university at the other end of the country.
We looked up the trains together, and I held back tears
as I realised I wouldn't be able to afford even the cheap-
est on my minimum wage Saturday job.
"It'll only be for the first year," he said. "Then you can
come and join me."
At seventeen, a year might as well have been forever.

"You shouldn't end up with the first boy that comes
along anyway," my friend Kelly told me, when I called
her, distraught. "It's not normal."
Everybody else seemed to feel the same way. My parents, my sister, and, most importantly, my friends. They
all talked about settling (which is 'bad') as distinct from
settling down (which is 'good').

So, we split up. I left college, I went out into the world, and I had my heart broken over and over, until I no longer resembled the person I had been when I was with him. I didn't settle for the first boy who came along. But I should have.

17.
The Storyteller

She had wanted it for her whole life. Everyone in her village did. Everyone in her family, especially, because there had been another Storyteller, three generations ago, and everybody knew that these things tend to run in families.

She was nineteen when she woke with a feeling of pressure inside her head, as if something was trying to burst its way out of her skull.

"Mother," she called, half staggering into the cottage's small kitchen. "I think something's happening to me."

She could hardly get the words out, hardly even think around the headache taking root in her mind.

The girl's mother took one look at her and sprang to her feet, spilling hot tea across the table.

"Quickly," she said to the girl's uncle. "Send to the temple for a scribe."

The scribes had only just arrived when the girl began to speak, the words bubbling up from between her parched lips. She talked for almost two days without eating or sleeping, while the scribes worked in shifts to record her words.

"Congratulations," they said, when she finally shuddered to a halt. "You are a Storyteller now, and you have brought great pride to your family."

She thought that she had understood what it meant to be among the chosen, but without the story to sustain her, she felt no triumph, only loss.

18.
The View from the Top

The room should have been pleasant at least. It was one of the most expensive rooms in an exclusive private hospital – the very best that money could buy.

The other patients had all decorated their spaces with drawings from their children or grandchildren, family photographs, flowers. But the man in room number 600 had nothing. Nothing to disguise the medical equipment or to brighten up the slightly spartan space, to make it seem more like a hotel and less like a hospital. Nothing to hide the fact that he had come here to die.

"You don't have any family you want me to call?" Anne asked as she made notes on his chart.

"No one who would come." His voice was strained, and it held that tell-tale rattle that she had come to recognise as signifying when a patient was running out of time.

"Even…" she began, and then stopped. *Even now*, she wanted to say. *Even at the end.*

In the corridor outside, a child laughed, and a voice shushed it gently.

The man in the bed turned away from Anne and fixed his gaze on the skyline, visible through the large window at the far side of his room.

"You're so insulated when you're at the top," he said. "Especially in a business like mine."

Anne had no idea what kind of business the man had been in, but she said nothing.

"You're soundproofed," he continued. "Cut off by people who only ever say 'yes'. You can get right to the end of your life before you realise that you can make a fortune, and still lose everything worth having."

19.
What's in a Name?

Everybody keeps calling her by the wrong names. At school, she's 'Mrs Preston' – a name that never quite seemed to fit. To her, it feels like trying too hard, as if she's a child balancing in her mother's high heels, just playing at being a grown-up. She would have preferred plain old 'Emma', even from her class, but it isn't the done thing. It's not how grown-ups operate.

Outside the school-gates her name has vanished entirely, replaced with 'mum' or with some version of it.

She's 'mum' to her children, frequently 'Mrs Callum or Sophie's mum' to her children's friends, and just 'Callum and Sophie's mum' to their parents. Even her husband has adopted the moniker, telling the children, "Your mum said no," if he's being supportive, or "Your mother doesn't want you to do that", if he disapproves or her choices.

Sometimes, lying in bed at night, she wonders how much of her is wrapped up in her old name, the one she never hears anymore. She's sure that she was somebody else once, back when there was still a small, quiet piece of her mind that held some essential part of her own nature. Before her life became a constant whirl of tasks, to-do lists and calls to action. Before she became an exile from herself.

20.
Homing Instincts

I think it must have been some animal part of me, some instinct for safety that caused me to head home just before the lockdown order was announced. Although 'home' had never before been a place that I'd associated with 'safety'.

The streets of my small town were already empty when I arrived. People had shut up shop and ebbed away, back to their protective bubbles, leaving me with only the ghosts of my younger self for company.

I bumped into them everywhere, these versions of me. As I passed the old park, I saw the ghost of myself at eight years old, swinging back and forth on the tyre swing, legs stretched and tiptoes just trailing in the dust. As I made my way through the streets at the back of my old school, the ghost of my eleven-year-old self marched past, singing an old Spice Girls song, defiantly at the top of her voice. As I passed the Star and Garter pub, empty and boarded up for years, sixteen-year-old me stumbled out and vomited, neatly, on the steps.

The closer I got to home, the more of me I encountered, until I started to keep my vision fixed firmly on my shoes. I had seen enough of the person I had tried to leave behind.

As I made my way along the garden path, I looked up to find the spectre of my nineteen-year-old self crouched against the front door, cradling herself, and weeping. She raised her head and made eye contact with me, scrubbing the last of her tears from her red-rimmed eyes.

As I reached out and took hold of the door knocker, she shook her head in silent warning.

21.
Daily Practices

"It's not fair," Andrea said. "We were going to do so much once you retired. We were supposed to go to South America together."

"Go anyway," Dave said.

"Without you?"

"Go for me." He pressed her plump hand between his two emaciated ones, his skin translucent and showing blueish veins beneath. "I want you to promise me you'll go. Don't just stop living because I'm not going to be around anymore."

Andrea squeezed his hand, gently. "I promise," she said.

She tried her hardest to keep her promise. She took the trip to South America that they had spent so long planning and, as she stood in the streets of Buenos Aires, she tried to picture him standing next to her, tried to imagine what he might say about the dancers in the streets or the view from the hotel. It only made her feel more alone.

When she came home, she tried to solve the puzzle of how to live without him. She joined groups aimed at widows and read books on bereavement, but nothing seemed to help. Eventually, she stopped talking, stopped reading. She stopped trying. She locked herself in, forgot about her promise, and waited to see what would happen next.

The soaring heights of joy and awe never returned.

Over the years, inspiration, serenity and hope all continued to slip away until she lived a life worn smooth by the daily practices of grief.

22.
The Liar

His stories used to drive me nuts. It wasn't just that they were untrue, it was that they were so blatantly untrue that I could never figure out the point of them.

Like the time when he was running late to meet me, so he told me that he'd witnessed a car accident and that he'd had to pull the driver out of the wreckage. Taken on its own merits, the story would have been unlikely but not impossible. The problem was that he told me a different version of the same story the next time he was late.

I could have questioned it, but in the end I decided to play along. It seemed easier than arguing.

When we reconnected years later, I had all but forgotten about his stories. Or perhaps I had remembered, but I'd told myself that we weren't kids anymore and everyone deserved a chance at reinvention. God knows, I wouldn't want anyone to hold my teenage indiscretions against me. And things were good, at first. I had almost forgotten how it felt to have someone tell me the things I most wanted to hear in the world – that I was pretty, that I was worthy. That I was loved.

But once a liar, always a liar. And although 'I love you' shouldn't sound so outlandish, from his lips it might as well have been a story about a car crash.
"I love you too," I said. Once an enabler, always an enabler, I guess.
"I'll never leave you," he said, and I imagined him with

one foot already out of the door.

"I believe you," I told him, precisely because I didn't.

I wanted to cling on for a little longer, but I knew the days were coming when he would make lies of all our truths.

23.
No Man's Land

Stephen had noticed the soldier in the line-up that morning. He couldn't have been a day older than thirteen – he was a head smaller than everyone else around him, and his thin shoulders were visibly trembling as he waited for instructions. He had taken half a step forward, intending to pull the boy out of the line and send him back to his parents, when he had forced himself to stop. There was no chance that the boy's commanding officer had failed to notice his age. At some point, someone had taken the decision to ignore their moral duty and send the child out anyway. Just another body for the battle-field.

It was too late now. For better or worse, the kid would be going over the top with the rest of them. He tried to find the solider again in the moments before the whistle blew, but in the crush of tense bodies, it proved to be impossible.

When the gunfire died down, he moved amongst the fallen, doing whatever he could to provide comfort, if not actual aid.

Over to the west he heard someone shout, "Medic!" and he made his way towards the shout, picking his way through the mud as it oozed around his ankles.

"He needs help," a voice said.

He moved the solider aside and looked down. It was the boy. He lay in the mud, his limbs splayed, and his face covered in blood.

Stephen swore and dropped to his knees. He pressed an ear to the boy's chest. Already he could hear his ebbing heartbeat, hear the slow hiss of air as it escaped from his lungs.

Around him, the wounded wailed piteously as the sounds of the battle moved into the distance. The melody of death.

24.
Folded

Every day she waited for a phone call, an email, a letter. Something to assuage her doubts – the doubts she didn't dare to voice.

Her friends all said, "You must be so worried about him," but she denied it. If she didn't give a voice to her anxieties, if she didn't give them any power, then maybe they wouldn't manifest.

She was in the living room, trying and failing to focus on the television, when she saw a shadow fall across the window. She looked up to find two men in suits making their way towards the front door.

Time seemed to freeze for long enough that she could make out every detail of them. The tall man with the greying hair, who frowned and brushed at some invisible speck of dust on his shoulder. The shorter man, younger and with an air of urgency about him that communicated itself in the way he darted his eyes, the way he pinched his lips into a hard, thin line.

An image of her husband flashed into her mind, lying in a hospital bed, wounded but alive, soon to be on his way back to her. She ran to the door and flung it open, a fearful hope clawing at her chest. One look at their faces was enough to drive her backwards, arms outstretched as if to ward off the truth. She didn't even hear the older man say, "I'm sorry," before she doubled over. A life folded in on itself.

25.
Christmas at the Lake

His footsteps are muffled, almost silent, and each movement sends a tiny flurry of snow into the air.

There was a moment when he thought that he might have lost the path, half buried as it was by both the snow and the passing of time, but then he recognised a birch tree, remembered the afternoon he had spent idly tearing at bits of bark, and all at once he knew exactly where he was.

Pushing through the trees, he finds the route and sets off once again. It's early when he reaches the lake, not long after dawn. The cold is biting his exposed face and sharpening his hunger. He has carried very little food with him, only a couple of slices of fruit cake, made to his mother's old recipe, some cheese, and a flask of coffee. In spite of the difficulty of the route, the cold, his hunger, he is determined to see in his last Christmas here, in what used to be his favourite place.

26.
Out of the Kitchen

"Shoo," my mother said.

She didn't say it the way my friends' mothers used to say it; there was no hint of humour in her voice. When my mother told me to get out of her kitchen, I made sure to get out of her kitchen.

My grandma used to let me bake cupcakes with her, but in my mother's kitchen she was the only person allowed to touch anything, except for the washing up, which I was expected to do, and do well.

I came home from school one day, aged around eleven, to find her lying on the sofa in front of some terrible day-time soap. She would never loll about on the sofa, and she hardly ever watched television, certainly not before the nine o'clock news. I think my jaw must have dropped as I saw her.

She cracked one eyelid open and regarded me with a single, bloodshot eye.

"A touch of flu," she said. "Nothing to worry about. Go do your homework."

I escaped to my room, where I struggled over my algebra and rushed through a history essay. When I had finished, there was still no movement from downstairs, and my stomach was beginning to rumble. I crept back down, and stared at her, unmoving on the sofa.

*Soup*, I decided abruptly. It was what she always cooked for me whenever I was ill and, thanks to a recent home economics class, it was one of the few meals that I had some idea how to cook.

Feeling almost like a criminal, I snuck into the kitchen, took out a knife and a chopping board and began cutting up peppers and onions.

The soup was already simmering when she came in.

"I was ... I thought," I stuttered. "I made soup," I finished lamely, sure that I was about to be punished.

Instead, she said, "I can see that," and sat at the table, watching me.

With shaking hands, I dished up two portions of soup, leaving the rest in the pan to cool. I set one of the portions in front of my mother and she stared at it.

"You haven't cut the vegetables into small enough pieces," she said, fishing out a chunk of onion. "The flavour isn't bad though," she added after she tasted a spoonful.

After that, she began to summon me regularly to the kitchen. She only ever spoke about the food – any attempt at deeper conversation, any personal questions and she would shut down. She made it very clear that she had no interest in getting to know me better and that I would be wasting my time if I tried to get to know her.

The smallest error, either in technical cooking skills, or in breaking her unspoken rules, would be enough to get me evicted and each time, I worried that she would refuse to take me back.

Once, early on, I added too much salt to a bread dough.

"No, no, no!" she snapped.

I reached for the bowl, but she snatched it away, scraping the dough into the bin.

"Can't take it back out now, can you," she said.

Almost thirty years later, I stood at her grave and watched as her coffin was lowered in. I'd wanted so badly to solve the conundrum of her, but no matter how hard I tried our relationship was only ever superficial. I thought it should have been easy for a daughter to connect with her mother, but now it was all too late. And as I threw a handful of earth on top of her coffin, I heard her voice in my head: *Can't take it back out now, can you.*

27.
Autopsy of a Relationship

We used to laugh at those couples who don't talk when they go to restaurants. We used to wonder why they bothered, why they didn't just give up when they clearly had nothing left in common anymore, nothing to hold them together.

Now I know. When you've bound your life to another person's life – kids, mortgage, years of shared history – it's no small thing to extricate yourself. It isn't as simple as just deciding to walk away.

I tried to figure out what was wrong. I kept asking, "Are you okay, is everything alright?"
And every time, he said, "Yes, I'm fine, everything is fine," in a way that told me to back off, stop pestering, give him space.

So now it's us sitting in the restaurant in silence, picking at the rapidly cooling food on our plates, as I wonder for the hundredth time where it all went wrong, what chance I missed to stop us from unravelling. But it's not in his nature to explain, and I'm too tired to keep asking.

28.
Torrent

I've worked hard to convince everybody that I've left my past behind me. I've worked hardest of all to convince myself.

After I got clean, I was still a mess. Twenty pounds underweight and covered in scars where the needles had left their marks up and down my arms. No job. No real education to speak of. No prospects.

It was a fight to re-make myself. People seem to think that it's simple, that you just slough off the dead cells of your old self and reveal the shiny new person underneath. But it isn't like that. It can't be like that when you can't manage to forget how it feels to fly on the days when you're not just tethered to the earth but actually sinking through it. It can't be simple, when the only people who will even look at you most days are the people who are just as broken as you.

Every day is a battle. And the moment when I think that I might have won is always when I'm in the most danger. The river of my past, of my mistakes, keeps flowing, a raging torrent ready to drag me in and sweep me away, until I'm so far from the person I want to be that I'll never find my way back.

29.
Grave Tidings

She almost missed it in the gathering dark.

"Turn right at the fork in the road, by the burnt-out inn," the old man had told her, and she had dutifully followed his instructions, ending up in a small clearing in what used to be the far end of a village.

There was a sense of foreboding in the air, and she pulled her cloak tightly about herself as she dismounted from her unusually skittish horse. Curiosity had brought her this far and it was curiosity that won out over fear as she drew closer to the rough mound of earth.

She could see where the ground had been overturned, the little grave emptied of all that had been within it. In spite of her view of herself as enlightened and rational, she made the sign of protection, her right forefinger raised above her palm as she traced the symbol through the air.

The grave's former occupant had been rumoured to be a saint. Tales of her miracles had spread far and wide, and travellers had journeyed from miles around to come to the little village, seeking to be cured of their illnesses, or seeking benedictions to bring them luck.

When the girl died after a short but brutal bout of the sweating sickness, the villagers buried her in a place where they believed her soul could still watch over them. It was a mark of respect in a place where they would usually have thrown her remains into one of the mass graves.

For a while, the pilgrims had still come to the village to pray at her makeshift shrine. To begin with, that seemed to be enough for them. But then the rumours started to spread, first that the saint had been buried with a great treasure, and then that the saint herself was the treasure, that her bones would bring luck to anyone who possessed them. It was inevitable, despite the villagers' best efforts to protect their saint, that someone would eventually appear who was too strong for them to fend off. When the raiding party came, they were almost thirty strong. They carried off the bones, and sacked the village as they passed through.

The rider's horse pawed the ground, restless, and she turned away from the pile of earth and from the small, sad marker stone that was all that remained of the village of Deuil and its fabled child-saint.

30.
Forgotten Places

The message had come through in the early hours of the morning. Two words, both capitalised: 'Get Out'. It came from an unknown sender, and she didn't bother to text back or to call the number. She knew that the number would have ceased to exist seconds after the message was sent, the SIM card already snapped in half, and probably flushed down the nearest toilet for good measure. The sender had done their job in warning her; they wouldn't stick around to check whether she acted on the information. Everything else was up to her.

She took the SIM card from her own phone and ground it to dust under her boot. She reached under her bed and pulled out a bag. It had been packed for days. Warm clothing, bottled water, cash, a little jewellery (it never failed to surprise her how willing people were to trade food or fuel for something shiny) and, tucked into the lining of the bag, ID in three different names.

The coordinates had been slipped under her door a week ago, and the car keys had been left sitting on the mat. The grabbed them both from the shelf where she had left them and made her way to the car park, without bothering to lock the door behind her as she left.

The car started first time. There was no satnav, only an old AA atlas sitting in the driver's side glove compartment, and she silently thanked every roadwork-infested trip she'd taken as a child, every time she'd ever acted as navigator for her father. She traced her finger along the route, memorising the first dozen junctions, and then pulled slowly out of the car park, watching for any movements, the way she had been taught.

The roads were quiet as she drove. She didn't see another soul until just after four in the morning, when she pulled into a twenty-four-hour garage to use the toilet and top up on fuel. The bored teenager behind the kiosk barely looked at her as she handed over the cash, and she did nothing to make herself memorable.

She circled the old motel once before she pulled the car onto a flattish patch of tarmac that looked as though it had once been a car park. There was no sign of life. Inside, the front desk was unmanned, and obviously had been for some time; the computer on the desk was ancient and the lights didn't switch on when she tried them. Her instructions had said 'room 112' so that was where she headed, careful not to touch the handrail on the staircase that looked as though it might fall away at the slightest pressure.

The door opened with a loud squeak, revealing a room with a clear view over the car park. The bed sheets were threadbare, and a mosquito lay dead on the pillow, its body plump with stolen blood. *Perfect*. Idly, she wondered who had lain here before her, and whether hiding in this forgotten place had saved them too.

# Part 3 -

# Curiosity

---

1.
A Penny for your Thoughts

Ella couldn't remember the last time her belly was full. What food she had been able to forage or steal almost all went to the little ones. Her greatest joy, even if they did eat more than she would ever have thought possible. They were growing fast, and every day she fancied she saw more of their father in them. It wasn't just their looks, it was in the way the girl spoke, the way the boy carried himself.

Sometimes Ella would watch them until her heart seemed ready to burst with the combination of grief and pride. Then she would have to turn away, to compose herself.

It was late when the witch came. Ella knew who she was, she had heard all the stories, but she was unprepared for the reality. She watched as the witch moved through the street, apparently oblivious to the people around her. Everyone moved out of her way, flinched back, as if afraid that the thin figure with her close-cropped hair would work some evil magic on them if they touched her.

As Ella watched, the woman froze and then, slowly and deliberately, sniffed the air, like a dog trying to catch a scent on the wind. Her eyes met Ella's and she grinned.

She crossed the street in a few long strides and stopped, too close to Ella for comfort. She sniffed again and closed her eyes, pleasure crossing her face, as though she had smelled an expensive perfume.

Ella was about to back away when the woman opened her eyes.

"Hello, my dear," she said, and her voice reminded Ella of the wind howling through broken glass; cold and harsh. "You have something very valuable there, you know."

Ella glanced back at her children, hiding behind her skirts, but the woman laughed. It was not a pleasant sound.

"Oh, no. Not them. What would I want with them?"

"What then?"

"Your husband."

"My husband is dead," Ella said, her anger overwhelming her fear.

"And it was a true love match too. His death brought you such pain." The woman inhaled again. "I'll buy it."

Ella frowned. "I don't understand."

"Your memories of your husband. I want to buy them, girl. I have coin in my pocket, see? Enough to feed you and keep your little family warm all through the winter."

Ella opened her mouth, but before she could speak, the witch put a hand on her shoulder and flicked her eyes to the two children.

"Don't refuse me," she said.

Still, Ella hesitated. "I'll lose my memories of him?"

The witch nodded. "And keep your children alive for another year in return."

"And what will you do with my memories?"

"Oh, my dear, you can't even imagine. I shall make mosaics from your tears and poetry from your pain. Your love will live forever in my work."

2.
The Lore of the Living

He doesn't know who lights the fires in the empty trash cans, only that they burn, without fail, every night. Overhead, on the bridge, he can see blue lights streak through the air, hear the scream of sirens split the night.

He can feel the change in the atmosphere long before they appear. He doesn't know how they find him, what it is about him that seems to summon them. He only knows that he will keep coming back to this place, night after night, and each night the lost ones will crawl from the darkness and gather around him.

Tonight, he hears them coming. Hears the rustle of stiff fabric, the whisper of voices and – worst of all – the wail of a child. He forces himself to remain where he is; he knows from long experience that he cannot leave until he has spoken with all of them, no matter how difficult it might be.

They crowd around him, and he feels the weight of their expectations.

"Let me tell you about yourselves," he begins, as always. Tonight, he will start with the child.

"You are a son and a brother. Your parents loved you very much and it made them happy to love you." He continues talking for some time. They boy does not interrupt.

Every night he comes here and waits for the lost ones. Every night he recites the lore of the living, tells the gathered souls about who they used to be. Comforted, they retreat back into the shadows. Alone, he tries in vain to remember anything about his old life.

3.
A Test of Courage

She has wanted this for as long as she can remember. She's studied hard, worked every spare moment, believing with every fibre of her being that one day she would be one of the lucky few who was invited to take the test.

The parchment itself was unremarkable when she pulled it out from under her door, but she knows as soon as she unrolls it that this is it. This is what she has spent so long working towards. It's covered in blue ink that dances in the candlelight, swirling and roiling into impossible patterns. With a gasp, she rushes to the small desk at the end of the room and pulls a looking glass out of the drawer. Laying the parchment flat on the desk, she holds the mirror over the top of it. The paper is still covered with nonsense scribbles but as she watches, the reflection rearranges itself into writing. Making a mental note of the time and place given in the letter, she watches as the images shift one last time, coalescing into the symbol of a skull and crossbones, before vanishing entirely from both the paper and the reflection.

She looks out of the window, checks the position of the stars and uses them to calculate the hours until midnight. Satisfied, she dons her cloak and sets off through the dark.

She checks the corridor twice, before she mutters the words of the spell under her breath. There. It's subtle but unmistakable, the slight glow of a glyph next to one of the identical doors. She lets out a breath and allows herself a small smile. She's passed the first two tests. And then just as quickly the smile slides from her face as she remembers the final image. The warning is clear. Even accomplished practitioners have died attempting these trials. She pauses just outside the room. From within she hears the soft murmur of voices, sees flickering light spill out into the darkened hall. She reaches out a hand and places it against the wooden door, hesitating as fear goes to war with longing.

4.
The Visitation

The whole world seemed to have been arguing for years. Were they real, were they coming for us, would they be a threat? TV stations and news outlets revelled in polemic debates, and entire areas of the internet became virtual no-go zones. Friendships were destroyed over the arguments they caused; families were split apart.

And still, no one seemed to want to speak about the most pressing point of all: if they were real, if they were coming, if they were a threat to us, there wasn't anything we could do to stop them.

In the end, there was no warning. One moment the brilliant blue summer skies were clear of anything but the occasional fluffy cloud, the next moment they were full of dark shapes hanging overhead. We stared up; all arguments forgotten - an entire world momentarily united in fear. Before anyone had time to react, the heavens lit up with a beam of blindingly bright light.

We shielded our eyes as it lanced across the sky. When it was over, the city was untouched and we thought perhaps that we had been wrong to be afraid, or that maybe we had somehow been spared. Until we started getting word from out of town. About how whole forests had burned to the ground, how rivers and streams had boiled dry, and about how, down on the shores, the heat had been intense enough to melt the sand into glass.

5.
Fallen Heroes

"He's a hero," Vyn said.

He laughed and there was bitterness in it.

"You think so? Look around - this group is made up of people who can take care of themselves. The witch, the assassin, the fighters. He isn't protecting anybody; he's just thrown in his lot with the group that gives him the best chance of staying alive."

"What about me? I'm not any of those things."

"What you are is a novelty. Some little innocent thing who thinks the world begins and ends with him. As soon as that novelty wears off, as soon as you become more trouble than you're worth to him," he added another log to the fire, sending sparks into the night sky, "your heroic warrior will leave you to fend for yourself."

They were silent for a moment and then he said, "You don't believe me? Where do you think he is right now?"

She followed his gaze to the small, dark tent with the painted symbols. The witch's tent.

He stayed in the tent until just before first light. Vyn watched him leave, something akin to grief clawing at her chest.

She was about to creep back to her own tent when she noticed movement and looked up to find the woman staring at down at her.

"You're together then?" Vyn said, as lightly as possible.

"We are."

"But aren't you worried about ..." she trailed off, but

107

her hands hovering just above her stomach made her meaning clear. Having a baby on the road would be notoriously dangerous during peacetime. During wartime, it would be a death sentence.

The woman threw back her head and laughed.

"Am I not a witch? Are we not famous for our ability to reave the potency from men?"

6.
History Project

What's this for again? Oh, your history project. And I just speak into this thing here, do I? Okay then. Well, I'm afraid you might be disappointed, because I don't really remember there being magic in the world. Not real magic anyway. I was only a kid when it left. Why did it leave? Well, no one knows that. There have been all sorts of theories over the years, of course, and I've lost track of all the times politicians and so-called 'entrepreneurs' have claimed to be able to bring it back. For a price, obviously. I do remember the night it went away though.

The light was so bright it woke us all up. We knew something was happening, but we had no idea what. Still, we rushed outside to see it - we were braver then, you see. Thought nothing of rushing outside in the middle of the night. Anyway, there it was: a thousand cascading silver stars fleeing into the night sky. It was the most beautiful thing I've ever seen in my life – even to this day. Even though I think we all knew that something sad was happening. There was this feeling of loss in the air, as if we knew that something precious was about to vanish.

But what I remember most vividly was the silence when it ended, and how cold we were as we huddled together in the snow in just our pyjamas and socks.

7.
Eclipse

The sky was already turning grey when I heard the stone hit the window. Startled, I looked down into Griff's grinning face.

"Coming out?" he asked.

"I can't. I promised my mother."

He snorted. "I didn't think you believed in all that superstitious crap."

"I don't." I was surprised to finds his words stung me.

"Then come on. This only happens once in a generation. Do you really want to wait until you're an old woman before you get to see it?"

I'd never thought about being an old woman before. I imagined by life passing me in a blur, and for a second I felt dizzy. It was only for a second though, and then my vision cleared, and Griff was still there, grinning that lopsided grin at me.

"Let's go," I said.

Clouds were gathering overhead as we made our way to the hill. I felt the disappointment course through me. What if we didn't get to see it after all? The wind rose and the clouds parted, giving us a momentary glimpse of the ring of light around the darkened sun. The weak glow wasn't enough to part the gloom. Next to me, I heard flint strike and I looked over just in time to see the flame ignite. Griff smiled, the reflection in his eyes mimicking the display in the sky.

8.
Lovelocked

It might have all been my idea, but I can't quite re-member now. I know that I was the one who'd read about it, but we were both excited to do it. I do know that it was me that fastened the lock to the bridge and you that threw the key into the river below. I still remember the way you laughed; that little flourish you made with your hand as you cast it away.

We watched the key sink as we swore our eternal love, sealing our promise with a kiss.

It was supposed to be nothing more than a romantic gesture, just a little bit of fun. We had no idea about what was listening or how our casual words had just bound us – and it – together.

There were no warnings. No rumble of thunder, no ominous peal of laughter. In fact, I seem to remember a perfectly pleasant day that ended with dinner and a movie and us, spent and curled up together in that old double bed you used to own.

Our last perfectly pleasant day.

I started seeing the creature out of the corner of my eye the next day. At first it was small enough that I could believe it was nothing serious, just a by-product of too much drink or too little sleep. But then came the day I caught you staring, the day you turned to me, ashen-faced, and asked, "Do you see it too?"

9.
The Memorial

She heard his goodbye on the wind. It struck her out of nowhere, a single discordant note on an otherwise tranquil winter day. All of the air seemed to leave her lungs in one great rush, and she bent double with the sudden pain of it.

When the worst of it was over, she allowed herself a moment of prayer, allowed herself to shed a few tears, and then she returned to her work. The mid-winter snows had already started to fall, the mountain paths would be impassable until spring, and the village would need her healing skills during the cold and dark months ahead.

At the first thaw she took leave of the mountain village and made her way down into the valleys. She walked, steadily and sadly, for months. Her destination was half a world away from where she started, so that the hum of early summer was already hanging in the air when she arrived.

They knew who she was as soon as she entered the village. Children hid behind their parents' legs, suddenly shy. Adults watched in silence as she passed, some of them bowing or making the traditional sign of respect. She nodded to each of them.

Eventually, she reached the centre of the village, the small council house. A man was already waiting for her, the robes of office settled on his shoulders.

"Welcome," he said. "We know why you are here."

He led her from the building and pointed to a path leading to a small hill.

"He was a sorcerer," the man said. "He spoke words of magic."

She felt the tears in her eyes. At the top of the hill was a small marker stone, half grown over with butter coloured flowers.

"A poor memorial," he began.

She shook her head. "It's perfect."

10.
The Freighter

I'd tried to play it cool as I sauntered through the lower hangar deck. I'd kept my head up, forced myself to move slowly. Anything to make myself blend in, to make it seem as if I had nothing to hide.

I shouldn't have bothered. Jake's contact took one look at me and laughed.

"Fifty credits," he said, holding out one scarred, grease-covered palm.

I opened my mouth to argue (old habits die hard, I guess), but he shook his head.

"Nah, I'm not lowering the price. Not even for Jake, so don't try playing that card with me. Your picture will be on every screen in the station by now, and it won't be long until someone notices you, even down here. You want transport off? It's fifty. Final offer."

I hesitated. It wasn't the price that bothered me, not really. Under the circumstances, I'd expected to be fleeced, and it could've been a lot worse. No, it was the name of his ship, 'The Sisyphus'. I couldn't decide whether it was a joke to name a freighter after a man whose eternal punishment was to push a rock uphill or whether it was just an inauspicious sign.

Still, beggars can't be choosers, as they say.

11.
The Way Home

A half-hidden path weaves in front of her and she wonders idly whether it's the summer heat that's making everything seem to shimmer and sway.

"Stay," the boy says, but she knows that she can't. She knows that it's time to go.

She holds out the sword and the boy takes it from her, almost reverently, labouring with the weight of it.

"Won't you need it?" There are tears in his eyes as her speaks.

"Not anymore." Her voice sounds strange, faraway somehow.

With the boy's help, she struggles to her feet. She smiles at him one last time, and takes her first faltering steps along the path, towards whatever lies beyond.

And something in the shadows seems to whisper, "Almost home."

12.
The Wheel Turns

It used to be different. Solstice nights used to be a celebration of the power of nature, of the turning of the year. We used to come together in this place of power and sing until the dawn. Some of my sisters would bring their children, someone would always be playing music or telling stories. The night would be filled with joy.

But that was before. Now the witchfinders have returned and only the bravest – or the most nihilistic – of us would dare to come out here anymore.

I feel my sisters out here with me, silent in the trees that encircle the stones. With an hour to go until the dawn, we rise as one and make our way into the stone circle. It's been a long, cold night, fraught with dangers, but I can feel the power and potency that rises with the sun.

Outside the circle, I can hear the shouts of the men, the baying of the hounds, but they've left it too late. Our power has already risen, and our rituals have begun. We join hands, join powers, and prepare for what comes next.

13.
Justice is Blind

It was a great honour, the greatest of any arbiter's life. And I thought I was prepared for it. They told me that my role as Oppositional Advocate meant that it was my duty to challenge every proposal put before me, that I would be the final step in the system of checks and balances that meant every plan would be judged solely on its merits instead of on nepotism or lobbying.

And maybe I made certain assumptions. Maybe in the back of my mind I thought that I could cheat a little bit, argue a bit harder against some ideas, smooth the way for others. After all, I'd spent my whole career on the other side of this, and it was only natural that I wanted to steer the conversation. It was what I assumed that everyone before me had done.

The day of my swearing-in ceremony, there was a knock on my office door. A smiling woman in a doctor's white coat led me to a small lab in the basement of the civic building.
"Just a routine medical," she assured me.
I didn't protest when she strapped me into the chair, although I couldn't tell you why. I didn't have time to question her before I felt a pinch. I looked down to find a needle in my arm.

It's the final, final step in securing our democracy. The step that secures it against the Oppositional Advocates themselves. The one that ensures you won't vote with your conscience, that you won't hold back some plans or support others.

But they don't tell you about the memory wipe procedure, they don't tell you that for as long as you do this job you won't remember what you believed before.

14.
Alone

I was nobody. A foot solider in a forgotten army, fighting in a long-forgotten skirmish. There was no reason for me to be spared.

And yet when I cried out, wounded on the battlefield, when I promised to dedicate my every breath, my every undying victory to any who would spare me, something did.

At first, I revelled in my new-found prowess. I was stronger and faster than I had been. I could fight for hours – days, even – and never tire. And I joined every army, fought for every cause that I could find. I played my part in revolutions and helped to change the course of history.

There were always a rare few who would discover my secret, who would envy my healing abilities, unending youth. But the truth is that the longer I've lived the more I've come to see that this so-called blessing is more of a curse. For who would want to spend an eternity living in the shadows, having to hide their true self? Who would want to be the only survivor or a battle, or an empire? Or of a world?

15.
Vanity

"Rowan, hurry. For the gods' sake, child, I'm four times your age, how is it that I can move with more haste?"

Rowan cursed under her breath as she kicked mud from her waterlogged boots. The storm was closing in fast, and the enemy army was bearing down on them almost as quickly.

Ramsay finally came to a halt, dropped his bag on the wet earth, and began digging through it.

"Damn. Our supplies are nowhere the near the level they should be."

Rowan let out a sigh, dropped her own pack, and rubbed at the place on her shoulder where the strap had been chafing at her skin.

"It's no surprise," she said. "We've been following the camp for weeks now with no time to re-supply."

"Yes, and look where that has left us," Ramsay snapped. "In dire straits and without the means to protect ourselves."

She was about to snap back at him, to remind him that he was the one who insisted it was their 'duty' to attach themselves to the King's Legions, to 'do their part', when he sighed and ran his fingers through his wet hair, always a sure sign of fear. She relented immediately, ashamed that she had failed to notice how exhausted, how afraid he was.

"Here," she said. "There must be something that can help us." She rifled through the pack, surprised to find a small, intricately decorated hand-mirror nestled amongst the vials and potions.

He took is gently from her, his gnarled fingers covering her own.

"That isn't for you. It's part of my spell-work. Sometimes all you can do is appeal to the vanity of the gods." His face broke into a smile. "You know, you may have something there, my dear. I think perhaps it's time for you to learn something new."

16.
Actions Speak Louder Than Words

The meeting has already devolved into an argument by the time I arrive, last as usual. I'm lucky enough to be able to sneak into the room and slip into an empty seat in the back. I don't know what's going on, but Lucy from HR is whispering furiously at Mark from accounting. She's practically sitting on her hands, she's so angry. Over on the other side of the room, one of the managers (the new one, I don't know his name yet) is riled up enough about something that his voice is almost audible, even from all the way over here.

Just when I'm starting to think that things can't get any more heated, one of the junior account execs picks up his copy of the meeting agenda and waves it in the air.

The noise is deafening.


(This story was originally published online as part of National Flash Fiction Day's 'Flash Flood' 2021)

17.
Walker of Worlds

He used to tell me all about his travels, almost from the first moment we met. Outlandish tales, but beautiful. And something about the way he spoke made me want to keep listening to him, even though I didn't really believe him. Not then. Not right away.

He told me that he was a refugee, that he was being hunted. I learned to live with his jumpiness in open spaces, his refusal to sleep anywhere outside his home, the constant sense that we had to be alert because 'people' might be coming for him, because the 'bad thing', whatever it was, might happen at any moment. It seemed, to me, to be a price worth paying.

When the 'bad thing' finally did happen, I didn't see it coming.

It was such a prosaic way to go. A drunk driver ran a red light and mounted the kerb. He had no time to move out of the way.

I cradled him in my arms, begging him to stay with me.

"Look at you." He was almost smiling, despite his injuries. "You're so human. You think if you just concentrate hard enough you can hold me here. But I've seen worlds where the air glows, and galaxies where the stars themselves sing. I'm not sorry to leave this tawdry place behind."

18.
The Colour of Darkness

"Try again"

I close my eyes and concentrate on calling my power, but I see nothing except the darkness rising around me. With a gasp, I open my eyes. "I think there's something wrong with the spell. I see shadows gathering every time I try it."

"That's your power coming as you call. Very good." She's smiling, but the smile fades as she sees my expression. "What is it?"

"My power can't lie in darkness. It's evil."

I expect her to shout, to be angry at my ingratitude but instead she crosses the floor and rests her hand lightly on my shoulder. I can feel her callouses through the thin material of my blouse.

"That's the belief you have been raised with, but it's too simplistic. Darkness is not evil, it's merely the absence of light."

"What if light is the absence of darkness?" I'm just being contrary, but she glances at me as if I've said something interesting before she shakes her head, her grey curls bobbing.

"No. Darkness is absence. It's space." She holds her hands out wide as if to demonstrate. "That's the point of it. Some practices require space."

I frown. "I don't understand."

"Here. Let me show you."

She takes my hands in hers and I feel our breathing fall into the same rhythm. The shadows seem to slip from the walls and pour across the floor towards us, pooling like ink at our feet. Now that I'm really looking, I can see the colours that swirl within their depths, like the blues and greens hidden in a magpie's feathers. It isn't fearsome at all. It's beautiful.

I hold her hand and look upon my darkness and for the first time I am not afraid.

(This story was originally published online as part of National Flash Fiction Day's 2021 anthology)

19.
Re-Set

I wake to the sound of a blaring alarm. My first in-stinct is to roll over on the sleeping mat, towards where you're supposed to be. But you're not there. I already knew it, I'd just forgotten. Again.

I push off from the sleep unit and I'm on my feet and running almost before my brain can catch up with what I'm doing. I almost forget that the most direct route to the control room is blocked by debris, skidding to a halt just as I come to corridor B.

*Which way?*

I know this, I know that I do. Why can't I remember?

*No time.*

Taking a chance, I turn left. I make it maybe thirty feet before a cable flares overhead, dropping in front of me in a shower of sparks. I duck, but I can feel the place where it's whipped across my cheek, burning a line into my skin. Worse still, I know it's slowed me down. I'll never make it to the control panel in time.

I try anyway, of course I do. I always try. But the emer-gency seals are already in place and there's no way through.

Your eyes are wide and frightened on the other side of the glass.

"I'm sorry," you mouth at me.

"I love you," I mouth back.

The tears blur my vision so that I don't have to watch you choke as all the air is sucked from the room. All I can do is replay the events of the last few minutes, trying to force the information into my brain before the loop resets.

Maybe next time I'll make it.

20.
The Thief

It started almost innocently. She told herself that she would only take what she needed to survive. At first, she was clumsy with her thievery, fumbling the bun she took from the baker's stall so that she dropped it on the ground and had to leave it behind as she fled, or earning herself a beating when she got caught trying to pick a pocket.

As she practised her skills, she learned to take a piece of fruit without looking at it, or to palm a few coins from an unsuspecting stallholder.

When she had enough that she could keep a roof over her head and food in her stomach, she began to turn her talents towards trinkets, jewellery, hair slides. Once, she took a bottle of perfume from a shop as she pretended to browse and found that she liked the scent so much that she stole two more bottles, being careful to slip them from different shops each time, wearing her nicest clothes, her prettiest jewellery so that the shop assistants never looked at her askance.

Later, her avarice unbound, she would pluck with practiced fingers at the things that really matter, stealing a little confidence from one person, a little happiness from another.

21.
An Education

It was late when they brought the boy into his study. The candles were starting to splutter, and the room was in dire need of some fresh air.

It was apparent that the boy hadn't come quietly. He had a darkening bruise on his cheekbone, and he was breathing hard as Roberts practically dragged him into the room.

"That will be all, Roberts, thank you." He said, continuing to write even as he watched the scene in front of him.

Roberts looked for a moment as if he might argue, but after a second's hesitation, he nodded and backed out of the room.

He took note of what appeared to be a bite mark on the big man's hand as he left, and he resolved to keep out of the boy's reach. He continued to write for a few more minutes, his pen working steadily as he dipped it into the inkwell and made smooth movements across the page. When he sensed that the boy was getting too restless for him to delay any longer, he looked up.

"Well," he said. "Caught mid burglary, eh. That was careless." He made a tsking noise through his teeth, and noted how the boy's faced reddened, how his fists tightened at his sides. "A talent for exploration is useful," he continued. "But we'll need to teach you discipline to go with it."

"You'll brainwash me, you mean," the boy said.

He put down his pen and steepled his fingers. "Is that

what they say about me? Interesting."

22.
Virtue

District Four. Known locally as the 'Virtue District'. It might sound nice, but don't be fooled. Virtue is one of the best places in the sector if you need information, but you'll leave with less in your wallet and less in your soul than you had coming in.

The bright, neon lights aren't enough to hide the grime of the place. It covers everything in a grey, greasy film. The streets, the people, they all reek of it. I feel contaminated just being here.

It doesn't take them long to descend on me. The new ones, hungry-eyed and desperate, shivering in their cheap, synthetic fibre lingerie. The true professionals - the ones who survived for long enough to claw their way to the top of the food chain – nicer dressed but dead behind the eyes. The pros are the ones who are better at hiding their feelings, better at pretending that this is all just a bit of fun. They'll cater to just about any tastes too - as long as you don't want to cuddle after.

I make my way through the streets, fending off the grubbier ones, ignoring the catcalls. It's been a while since I was last here, but I remember my way. When I get where I'm going, the light above his door is already flashing, but I don't have time to wait. I knock. Hard.

"Rox," I shout. "You in there? I need you. Now."

It's another couple of minutes before his door opens and his customer sweeps out. Anywhere else in the system and she would at least have had the good grace to look embarrassed, but here she just looks angry.

"Hello, beautiful." Rox is thinner than the last time I saw him, all sharp angles set off against his electric blue hair. "Business or pleasure?"

"Information," I say.

"Oh, information. Well, that'll cost you extra."

He beckons and turns away, doesn't even bother to check that I'm coming before he returns inside.

I grit my teeth and follow him. This had better be worth it.

23.
The Well

Each day for a hundred days, the villagers have dropped a single, glittering coin into the well at the centre of the village.

In the dark of the new moon, she ties a bucket to a string and lowers it over and over, until she has collected each of the coins. Barefoot, she moves through the night, her feet making no sound on the soft grass, until she reaches the small cottage on the outskirts of the village.

Humming quietly, she digs ten rows in the loamy earth and plants ten coins in each of them.

The days pass and the plants begin to grow. Their small, silvery blossoms open in the light of the full moon. At midnight, she harvests the flowers, laying them in a basket as she works. At the end of the night, each flower releases a puff of fragrant, white dust, before curling into the shape of a half-moon. Each one of them is a spell, a blessing.

She counts her blessings and gathers them carefully. Each one is a tiny link in the chainmail she places around her heart. Protection against the encroaching dark.

24.
The Sound

The noise was so distracting. He wished he could cover his ears, block it out just for a moment, but his arms were strapped to the cold, metal table. He held tight to the images in his mind. *A woman in a white dress, smiling. A baby crying. A little girl on a bicycle, pigtails flying.* These were the things he knew to be important, even if he couldn't quite remember why. The things he needed to repeat to keep them fixed in his mind. *Woman in a white dress. Baby crying. Girl on a bike.*

The woman in the white coat leaned over him.

"Still fighting, I see," she said. "This will be so much easier on you if you just relax."

For a moment her face seemed to blur with that of the other woman's, the one in his memory. Was it a white dress she had been wearing or a white coat?

*Woman in ... something. Baby crying. Little girl on a bike. Or was it a little boy?*

"Increase the resonance," the woman in white said.

From the corner of his eye, he saw a figure move towards a console.

*Woman in a white coat, smiling. Boy on a bike. Dammit, what was the other thing?*

The sound grew until nothing else existed, until he could feel his sense of self start to dissolve. He cast around for something he could use to anchor himself; a face, a name, anything.

The woman in white waited impassively until she

saw his eyes dim, his jaw slacken.

"He is ready," she said.

25.
The Spaces in Between

We are the creatures you see from the corner of your eye; the second glance in the mirror, that half-remembered dream you can't quite hold onto upon waking. We are the faint sound of a lullaby in the distance, the scent of lilac on the breeze.

We live in the spaces in between. We exist in the moments between heartbeats, between breaths. Each cut, cleave or kerf out of time is our home and our playground. A space for our endless wandering.

We are older than the oldest among you, older than your entire world. Older than your concept of time itself.
And we are going nowhere.

26.
Convictions

Orange jumpsuited in the style of every prisoner dating back to the old Earth days, the line moved forwards, hampered by the chains around their ankles.

"It's a bit much, don't you think?" one of the men said. "We've already got the tracking chips in our necks, why do we need the chains as well?"

"Because, Reeves," one of the guards said, "the public like to watch prisoner transports and they can't see a chip, but they can see those chains. Makes 'em feel safe in their beds at night." She gestured to the viewing gallery.

He looked up and realised she was right. The little procession had drawn quite a crowd.

"Now, are you going to keep your mouth shut or," she placed one hand on the baton hanging at her waist, "should we really give them a show?"

"No, ma'am," he said, forcing a smile. "I wouldn't want to frighten the children."

She looked almost disappointed as she resumed patrolling the rest of the line.

They moved slowly through the ship, until they reached the stasis chamber. One by one, the men were unlocked from the chain gang, and then immediately locked into their stasis pods.

Upright, of course, Reeves noted. That way the company can fit in more passengers per trip.

Some of the men cried quietly as they waited to be put to sleep. A few shouted or made threats. The guards dealt with those ones.

Reeves waited for his turn, taking the opportunity to stretch as much as his pod would allow. He watched as the medics moved down the line, their equipment neatly stashed on a small trolley that they pushed along in front of them. When they were close enough, he watched the lead doctor speak to each man, before injecting him with a greenish liquid. Technicians followed the medical team, sealing each prisoner into his pod. It looked, to Reeves, practised and efficient. He was almost impressed.

"Any requests for you dreams?" the doctor asked.
"Dreams? But I thought -"
"You're going to be in stasis for over a decade. A mind with nothing to focus on will atrophy."
He hesitated. "There was a girl once."
The doctor nodded and Reeves felt cool liquid fill his veins as her face filled his vision.

27.
Lattice Work

Diane's eyes were gritty with lack of sleep. Her back ached from walking and her fingers burned where the rope had slid through her hands over and over again.

The last coil of rope sank to the ground and buried itself there, transforming into a glowing, golden line.

*Surely*, she thought. *This time.*

"No, no, no." The old woman's words were peevish, but her voice was strong, without even the hint of a quaver. "Look here. And here, again." She tapped the ground with her walking stick as she spoke. "You cannot afford to be shoddy with your spell-work," she scolded.

Diane examined the intricate lattice pattern carved into the wet earth. "I almost got it right."

The woman sniffed. "Almost isn't good enough. You have no idea what you might call forth by mistake."

28.
Acts of Desperation

The fever had burned for days with no end in sight. His sister could no longer be roused from her sleep, could no longer be given food. It was all the family could do to keep her from boiling alive, wrapping her in wet blankets to try to reduce her temperature, while she cried out and struggled against them, as if her fever-induced night-mares had transformed them into demons. She burned through the blankets almost as quickly as they could soak them.

Every time they held her down, the boy feared that they would accidentally crush her bird-like frame. Every time they forced water down her parched throat he feared they would accidentally drown her.

It was an act of desperation, trekking out to the edge of the forest where the cunning woman lived. The door opened before he'd knocked; she cut him off before he spoke.

"Sit." She pointed at an upturned stool nestled among the piles of papers on the floor. "I know why you're here, boy."

He was too tired, too afraid to feel any surprise.

"I haven't got any money."

"I know that too."

"Will you help us?"

She looked down at him. She was not tall, but as he squatted on the small stool, she fairly towered over him.

"What will you give me?"

He started. "I just told you ..."

"You don't have any money, I know. Who said anything about money? I asked, 'what will you give me' to save your sister."

"Anything," he said.

To his surprise, she laughed - a short, sharp sound that reminded him of a dog barking.

"Do you know where you are?" she asked him. "Do you understand what it is to make a promise like that to someone like me? No," she said, as he opened his mouth to speak. "Take a moment. Think about what I might ask of you. And then make a better answer. A shrewder answer."

He looked her in the eye and then, very clearly, said, "Anything."

29.
Remnants

I trudge through the dust, head down, face shielded. This street used to be the centre of the town, used to have cafes on the pavement and markets on a Saturday. Or so I've heard. I've never seen any of these things myself, but I can picture them just as if I was there.

The wind rises, carries more detritus towards me and I pull my scarf tighter around my face, close my eyes and wait it out. When the wind drops, I look down and realise it's blown something against my shin, something papery that curls and twists in the dying breeze. I reach down and unpeel it, wipe off the worst of the dirt. A ten dollar bill. I've never seen one before, but I know what it is. Mama made sure we knew the basics; she was so sure the old times would come back. I study it for a moment and then let the wind take it away. It's no good to anyone now.

30.
The Dress

The stitching on the gown was too fine for human hands. Fae then? It was the most likely explanation for its presence in her chamber. Certainly, her maid would not have laid out such a garment for her to wear. It was short, almost girlish in length, and patterned in pale green, in contrast to the heavy, dark brocade gowns that were fashionable this season. The stitching itself was in a thread that seemed to shimmer and shift colours as she stared at it.

Alyssa knew better than to touch anything made by the Fae. No matter how inviting it might be to dress herself in something so light, something that spoke to her of speed and movement. Of freedom.

She started to turn away, to call someone but, as if her hands acted of their own accord, she seized the dress and pulled it over her head. It was a perfect fit. Delighted, she watched her reflection in the mirror and, as she watched, the chamber door opened behind her, and her maid entered.

She took one look at Alyssa and screamed, rushing to her young charge, and attempting to pull the dress back over her head.

"Stop," Alyssa cried. "You'll tear it.

But the dress did not tear. And no matter how she pulled at it, the maid could not remove it.

A seamstress was brought in to try to unpick the threads, but each time she tried, they seemed to dance away from her, and she could not catch hold of the ends.

In her frustration, she tried to cut the dress apart, but the fabric only blunted her scissors.

With no choice but to leave Alyssa in the gown, they locked her in the chamber and left her to sleep.

All night long, she dreamed the dreams of wild things. She saw herself running through the woods, swimming in the rivers, and leading a group of green-garbed warriors to the gates of the castle.

And in the morning, when she awoke, there was a bracelet lying on her bedside table, the metalwork impossibly fine.

# Part 4 -

# Anger

---

1.
The Debt

It has taken years for Gabriel to execute his plan. When his village was ransacked by the hordes, right after harvest season, he had done his utmost to get himself taken away, ignoring his mother's weeping at the loss of her second son in as many seasons. Once he had been processed as a slave, he made sure to keep his head down, to be no trouble to anyone. He remained expressionless as he was kicked, shoved or spat at by his captors; he watched, impassive, as his fellow slaves were whipped for their real or their imagined infractions. The loyalty he owed to the living was nothing compared to the debt he owed to the dead.

He learned too, to make himself invisible so that he could access almost any room in the sprawling complex without challenge. So it was that he was unchallenged when he took berries from the bushes in the garden, or when he scraped ashes from the fire in the great hall, or wiped up pig's blood and salt, spilled on the floor in the kitchen. Or, riskiest of all, when he cleared the table after one of the general's feasts, stashing one of the goblets in an alcove so that he could retrieve it later.

The goblet was the final item he needed to carry out his plan. He wiped it out on one dirty sleeve, and took it to the kitchen.

"The general wants wine," he told the cook, a skinny man with a perpetually harried expression.

The cook filled the goblet without even looking at Gabriel and waved him away.

146

When he climbed the stairs to the general's study with the wine balanced on a tray, the guard at the door let him inside without question.

The general looked up from her book as he entered, bowing respectfully.

He placed the goblet in front of her and she picked it up and took a long swig, without acknowledging him.

Gabriel smiled for the first time in years.

The general looked up at him, at the expression on his face, and asked, "What are you looking at?"

"At a dead woman," he replied.

She opened her mouth to reply, but before she could speak, a coughing fit overtook her.

"It's an old recipe from my village," Gabriel said. "The village you destroyed two years running. The one where you had your people set the fire that killed my brother. There is no cure."

With an effort she gasped, "Fetch me a confessor. I must die with a clear conscience."

He leant down and leered over her. "With all the evil you've committed, do you really think one little prayer will balance the ledger? No, my lady. My village burned for days, but you are going to burn for all eternity."

2.
Here, There, Everywhere

Here:

I just wanted to keep you with me for as long as possible. I saw the way you looked at those posters, the way you idolised the heroes in those stupid films - the ones that were little better than propaganda. I told myself that it was just a phase, that all little boys go through it.

But I just wanted to convince you to stay. If I could keep you here, then I could keep you safe.

There:

You called us at first, of course. Your 'strong sense of duty' was wide enough to include your duty to us. All the same, we weren't surprised when your calls became less frequent. We knew you were busy, and we told ourselves it was a good thing, it meant you were settling in. Even when we stopped hearing from you altogether, we could convince ourselves for a little while that you were okay, you were just busy, out there somewhere.

Everywhere:

I see you all the time now, the way you used to be, before they took you away from me. I see you in the pictures hanging on the wall, and in the faces of the children I pass on the street. I see you around every corner, laughing on every park bench, smiling behind every window. My brave, beautiful boy.

(A version of this story was originally published online as part of National Flash Fiction Day's 'Flash Flood' 2021)

3.
Overwatched

"I have to leave," you told me. "There are matters else-
where that require my attention."

I held myself stiffly, while you kissed my cheek.

"I would prefer to take you with me, of course. But you
understand why that is impossible." You smirked, and it
was all I could do to sit still, to keep my eyes away from
the trunk in the corner of the room. The one where you
stored the dresses you like me to wear on 'special occa-
sions'. The trunk where I've hidden everything I've
managed to steal.

While you were away, I changed. You left others in
your place, of course, but they aren't you. With strict or-
ders not to touch me, they didn't see the point in
spending any real amount of time with me. They didn't
bother to watch me the way you would have.

And I used the time, I used your absence, to sharpen
both my wits and my stolen weapons against your return. It's almost time. And I will be ready.

4.
An Anniversary

The doorbell rings and I check the camera app. There you are, right outside my door just like I knew you would be. I know without checking that you have a plastic bag full of warm beer, the same way I know you'll have a mouth full of excuses.

Really, I don't understand how you could think that I would be surprised to see you. You come around every year, like clockwork. The seventeenth of July. The anniversary of your dad's death. The (much more recent) anniversary of the day that I decided I'd had enough of bearing the brunt of your anger.

The first couple of times you turned up, I let you in. I drank warm piss-weak beer with you, while you fed me every line in the book, and then, at the end of the night, I watched as you backtracked over everything you'd just said, while you explained why it would never work out between us. As if I was the one who invited you over.

By year three, I'd started texting you beforehand, asking you not to come. You sent me a string of angry messages back - and then you turned up anyway.

By year four, I'd changed my number, blocked you on social media, and set my emails up so that anything you sent me would bounce back unread. I'd left you with no way to contact me. You turned up anyway, and you'd already started on the beer before you started hammering on the door. When I let you in, I warned you it was the

150

last time.

So, this year, you can stand out there for as long as you like. Go ahead; I hear it's going to rain tonight. You can get drunk, kick my door, call me all the names under the sun.

Because I'm not there.

I half-smile at the app, and then turn the setting to 'mute' before slipping my phone back into my bag.

"Sorry," I say to my friends. "Another drink?"

Maybe you'll spend all night standing outside my door, maybe you'll eventually get bored and go home, maybe one of my neighbours will get fed up and call the police. It doesn't matter to me. You're not my problem anymore.

5.
Feathers

She did all the things she was supposed to do. Took every pill, went to every appointment, ate all the healthiest, most expensive foods, and always, always, always thought positive. As if all that positivity could repel the disease. As if even a whiff or fear or anger, or any kind of negativity at all, would cause it to expand, to colonise yet more of her body.

She was completely prepared for her good news. She had even practised her speeches in front of the mirror, tailoring each one for a different audience - family, friends, her support group - so that it would be appropriate and meaningful for everybody.

She felt good, she felt strong. She felt positive. So, she was completely unprepared for bad news.
"There's no hope," the doctor told her. "We've tried everything. I'm so sorry."

Rage bubbled up inside her. Every moment of positivity melted away. Every dark thought she'd tried to suppress coalesced into one single, black mass.
She let out an inarticulate growl and doubled over as she sprouted wings, not of feathers but of steel. Her wrath became a flaming sword, to lay waste to everything in her path.

6.
Rose-Tinted

You were younger than me, so it was my job to protect you. You got to enjoy your childhood. You got to have friends, and go to parties, and play with dolls. Sometimes you would greet me, wide-eyed and beaming as you told me stories about your imaginary world and the adventures you would have there.

Meanwhile, I fell into bed, exhausted, each night. I dropped out of college so I could work overtime - anything to make enough money to get us out. I didn't even have the energy to live in one world, and there you were, getting the best of two worlds.

Sometimes I think that maybe I didn't really do you any favours in the end. Because my callouses might have hurt me at the time, but my hard-earned cynicism will keep me safe. And you're still trying to live in your own world - as if the world I built for you wasn't enough.

You've always seen everything through rose-tinted glasses. As if harmless grandmas in quaint old cottages only want to offer you cookies and lemonade. As if that wolf howling in the woods is just a lost puppy. Who am I to take that away from you? You'll learn, on your own, soon enough.

7.
The Way We're Raised

I blame you for this. For all of my worst mistakes. For teaching me that I was worthless, that I should learn to accept any attention that came my way - no matter what strings were attached. That if a boy pulled my hair in the playground, it meant he liked me. Don't complain, you're not the most likeable person, take the attention where you can get it.

It's a cliché isn't it, blaming your parents? But those of us who were taught as children that the love we are entitled to is dependent on us being

quiet
        compliant
                good

often struggle with the idea that we are enough, just as we are.

8.
Isolation

It's difficult to explain why a man looking at you can fill you with fear. How, as a woman, you become familiar with the different flavours of fear; the stranger on public transport, the footsteps in the dark, the men who think that they have a right to your attention. It diminishes over time, the fear, but it never really leaves you.

We've all heard the stories, the whispers about the things that happened to a friend of a friend or to a colleague's sister. We've all shared the recipes for survival: "Remember to text me when the taxi drops you off" or "Don't walk home in the dark by yourself." We carry these stories, carry the precautions around with us, like a collection of protective talismans.

It's why we choose 'safe' places to spend our time. Like this place.

Except that now it doesn't feel safe anymore. There's been something strange about the atmosphere since the man in the black t-shirt arrived in the gym. It's emptying fast and everything seems somehow muted.

As if they sense the change, a group of women chattering by the hand-weights slowly descend into silence, until one of them says, "Shall we?" and indicates the door. The last woman to leave looks back at me, just as the door swings shut, and I realise that she's seen us – me and the man – that she's sensed that there's something going on. And at the last minute she's found a way to signal to me, to make sure that I'm aware of the danger.

It's time for me to leave.

155

And just as the thought enters my head, I sense movement beside me. There are three other treadmills in the gym, all of them empty, but he's chosen to use the one next to me.

"Your incline is all wrong," he says, leaning over me.

"I'm fine," I snap.

"I'm only trying to be nice."

"I don't need you to be 'nice', I need you to leave me alone." I'm so tightly wound that the words are out of my mouth before I realise what I'm saying. I feel oddly relieved though, as if I've been holding my breath and I've just let it all out.

I bring the treadmill to a stop and climb down.

He mirrors my movements and blocks my path, smiling.

I back up and he follows, staring at me, one eyebrow raised, amusement plain on his face: the same expression I've seen on every man who's ever threatened me. His face fills my vision and the fear and anger threaten to overwhelm me.

I reach behind me, and my fingers find something solid, a dumbbell left on the rack. I'm not even grasping for civility anymore – civility has never been any help. Instead, I surrender to the animal part of myself; she knows what to do, she knows how I can survive this.

(This is an edited version of a story that was awarded first place in its group in Round 1 of NYC Midnight's Short Story Contest 2021)

9.
Weak

He tore me apart and used everything against me.

My voice, which had started to shake whenever he stood too close to me, made me sound 'little' and 'weak'. My clothes, which I had always taken such pleasure in, made me a 'slut'.

One by one, the pieces of me fell away and left the core of me naked and exposed.

But when he grabbed my hair and used my ponytail to slam my head against the car - that was the first time I realised that nobody was going to come and rescue me, no matter how hard I screamed. It was the moment I knew that I was going to fight back.

10.
The Handler

It's past time for me to deal with this. I should have known better than to mix business with pleasure, especially in a line of work like mine.

It's been fun, this little diversion, but it needs to stop. No matter how badly he's going to take this, or how much it impacts our working relationship, the truth of the matter is that he's just too valuable as an asset to take the risk of this situation turning messy.

The place is a good choice for what I need to do. It's public enough that he won't be tempted to make a scene, but quiet enough that I can make an easy getaway if I need to.

It's clear from his expression that he's expecting trouble. Good instincts. It's part of what makes him so good at his job. He sits opposite me, unsmiling.

"I won't string this out," I tell him. "We'll carry on working together, assuming you don't request a different handler, but our personal relationship is done."

"I never loved you anyway," he says, and I can see on his face that he expects this to poleaxe me, to destroy me.

Instead, I take a slow sip of tea, pleased that my hands don't shake, and then I force myself to sneer back at him, "Idiot. This was never about love."

11.
Recipe for Disaster

You took your time perfecting your recipe for my destruction.

First, you added a little honey for sweetness, just to keep me coming back for more.

Then, chicory for bitterness, to balance out the sugar, and to remind me that there would always be something wrong in our relationship, there would always be a cloud in every sunny sky. And it would always be my fault.

Finally, the spice. The kind of heat that seems manageable at first. The kind that sneaks up on you, and builds to the point where it's all you can taste. Where it makes your eyes water and your guts churn. The kind you fear, unchecked, might lead to actual harm.

I wonder whether you smiled as you mixed your poisons. Did you enjoy watching me suffer as I ate up everything you gave me?

12.
The Troll Hunter

Kandygurl201: This is a little story that I hope will illustrate why women sometimes panic if they see you walking behind them on a night. I was walking home from one work one night when I passed a group of men hanging around outside.

One of them walked away from his friends and down the street after me. He was shouting at me to turn round and talk to him. I didn't know what to do so I started to run and he chased me.

When he caught up to me he pushed me over and he started grabbing at me. I was screaming the whole time and he must have thought that someone would come out of one of the houses because he told me to shut up, and then he hit me, and then he just stopped and left me there on the ground.

It's made me afraid to be outside on my own, especially if I see groups of men. I feel like I'm always looking over my shoulder.

HiyRez: It's not all men. Some of us are nice.

Errlybard: She didn't say it was all men.

HiyRez: She literally said she was scared of all men now. I'm sick of women pretending that we're all just waiting to rape them.

Errlybard: WTF is wrong with you? Someone shares a story about this horrible thing that happened to them and you make it all about you?

HiyRez: It probably never even happened. Look at her profile pic. No one would rape her. They'd have to kill themselves after.

Kandygurl201: Blocked.

Errlybard: Same. Blocked and reported.

Ramona read the last of the messages, gritted her teeth, and clicked on HiyRez's username. She scrolled through his most recent posts and sighed. *I'm going to need a beer for this,* she decided.

Two hours on the message board finally gave her a first name and a vague location. It wasn't much to go on, but it was enough to lead her to Facebook, where she spent some time looking through accounts matching those details. His account, when she found it, was locked down pretty tightly (smart), but he was using a similar profile picture to the ones he used on his other social media (less smart)

Armed with a full name and location, she trawled through local media and public records until she found what she was looking for.

"Hello, Thomas Evans," she said, smiling bitterly.

She hit the print key, finished her third beer, and climbed into bed.

A week later, Thomas Evans stood in his kitchen and opened a plain, white envelope, with his name and address printed neatly on the front. *No stamp*, he noticed, idly.

He pulled out the single sheet of paper and unfolded it. It was a printout of part of an exchange from a message board. At the top someone had scrawled in black marker, "Now you have to look over your shoulder too."

13.
Adoration

It was my own fault for trusting you. I should have known better - after all, I was certainly no love-struck teen. Except that you and I had been friends since the days when we were both love-struck teens, and every time I saw you, it felt as if I had been transported back to those days.

It had seemed like fate when we were finally both single at the same time. As if, after more than a decade of circling each other's orbits, gravity had finally pulled us together. I was still hurting a little from the last guy, and maybe I should have waited, taken some time for myself before I leapt into something with you, but you always made me feel safe.

You told me, "I'm afraid I'll hurt you", and I smiled and assured you that you wouldn't. We had been friends for so long and been through so much together that I couldn't imagine a world where our easy intimacy wouldn't translate into romance.

I should have known better. I should have remembered all the stories you used to tell me, about how you broke up with your last partner because she was too needy, the one before that because she was too controlling. They were all crazy, it seemed, and none of it was ever your fault. I should have stopped to consider the common factor. But by the time I came to you I was bloodied and bruised by my past failures, and I'd committed the cardinal sin of needing you. Too late, I realised my mistake. My adoration was no match for your scorn.

## 14.
### Bedtime Stories

The boy finally fell asleep some time after she'd finished telling the third story. She'd watched his eyelashes flutter as his eyes closed, watched his lips part as his breathing deepened. She lowered her voice, but carried on speaking, drawing out the moment for as long as she could. In the stories she wove for him, heroes fought great battles, and love conquered all. She spun her tale as one final gift to him before she had to leave.

In the corner of the room, her sword stood ready. The light from the dying fire reflected off the polished metal, illuminating the corners of the room. She'd had to stop the boy from playing with it earlier in the day, and even this had felt like a betrayal.

She heard the thunder of the horses' hooves as they approached, and she knew she was almost out of time. She looked again at the boy, still sleeping beside her, and raged, silently, about the unfairness of it all. But there were battles she must fight, and she knew he would be safer without her.

## 15.
## Duty

The hordes had come from the west, travelling through the last of the warm weather, and making their camp for the winter, almost within striking distance of the city.

The conscription calls had come soon after. Every man with a sword, an axe, or even a scythe to their name was ordered to report for training.

"Don't go," Rhia told her husband. "Stay here with me. They won't check every house; they can't find everyone."

"It's my duty to go."

"Duty be damned!" she threw down her ladle and it landed on the table with a thud that reverberated around the small room. "You imagine the glory and splendour of fighting for your king, but the truth of it is that you mean nothing to him, and everything to me. Out there, you'll die forgotten in some muddy field with the rest of them."

He looked for a moment as if he hated her. And in the morning, he left without a word.

16.
Pieces of Me

"You never support me," you say.

That's all it takes, just that specific accusation, and I'm seven years old and back with my mother again. *"You're a horrible little girl, it's no wonder nobody likes you."*

Reverting to form, I grasp for something to shield me from the horror of being unlikeable. I settle for 'helpful'. That sometimes worked on my mother.

"What do you need?"

"I don't know!" Your fists are clenched now, knuckles white against the dashboard.

I eye them warily but continue to speak anyway.

"No really, what do you need? What can I do?"

You suck in air, and when you expel it your words come out with it, all in a rush, as if you have to get them out right this second.

"Wait, slow down," I say, pulling out my phone and opening the notes app. I'm trying to make a list, trying to help, trying to be good.

You don't stop talking. I stop asking. I just nod, and note down what I can, hoping you'll forget about the rest.

"I love you to pieces," you tell me when it's over.

And I think, *Which pieces? Which pieces of me do you love? Is it my voice – the one you want me to stop using? My emotions – the ones you find inconvenient? Or my history – the one you've just re-written to score a cheap point in an argument? What pieces of me are you talking about? Without those things, what's even left of me?*

167

17.
Confession

Lilly was fifteen the first time she killed somebody. It was self-defence and almost accidental. Almost, because although she had thought about it, even pictured it, she hadn't really expected to go through with it. Once she realised that he was really dead though, she didn't waste a moment on regretting it. Instead, she celebrated her new and unexpected freedom by drinking what was left of the old man's whiskey, taking what was left of his cash, and jumping on the next train heading north. She had always wanted to try her luck in one of the big cities, and now there was no one left to stop her.

The second time was the man in the park. He'd followed her through the dark, heavy-breathing and laughing to himself. She didn't run. Instead, she took her time, found something she could use as a weapon, and waited for him. She waited until he was close enough to leer at her, to purse his lips and make grotesque kissing sounds, and then she swung the branch with all her strength, aiming at his head. He crumpled without making a sound.

She thought about going through his pockets, but in the end she couldn't bring herself to touch him. She hefted the branch into the duck pond, triggering irate squawking from its residents, and then walked away, leaving the body for the police to find.

It was only the third kill she really regretted. The man had just been in the wrong place at the wrong time. Plus, it was this third kill that got her caught. Third time un-lucky, she supposed.

Later, Lilly will speak of these transgressions - to therapists, and social workers, to her fellow inmates - and each time she will watch their faces carefully, scanning for signs of their shock, their anger, their understanding. Her weaponised honesty will tell her who she can trust.

18.
The Café

The relationship had been over for weeks and we both knew it. It had turned into a kind of competition between us as to which one of us was going to be the first to admit it.

She must have gotten fed up with waiting to have the discussion though because the next thing I knew, I was hearing from friends that they'd seen her around with this person or on a date with that one. She didn't even have the good grace to wait until we were officially over before she moved on. Or maybe she was trying to force me to break things off, to make me out to be the bad guy.

Eventually, she called and suggested lunch at our favourite little café. It was the place where we'd first met, the place where we'd spent so much of our time together.

She was late, leaving me to look like an idiot, sitting there, waiting for her. When she did finally arrive, she looked better than she had in ages - her hair was curled and put up in one of those fancy styles that women wear when they're trying to be impressive, and her lips were painted in a bright red colour. She looked better than she ever had when she'd been dating me.

"Hi," she said, kissing me on the cheek. "Thanks for coming."

I think I muttered something back.

"Coffee?" she asked. "Something to eat?"

I shook my head. The food here is my favourite, but I

was so full of recriminations that I had no room for anything else.

19.
Silence

They say that silence is golden, but my mother's was of the venomous, weaponised kind. A gloomy hush that spread over the house and rendered all of us voiceless in its wake.

It took me years to find my voice, but once I did, I made sure to use it at every opportunity. I spoke up at every protest, and added my name to the bottom of every petition. I started newsletters and newspapers, wrote websites and blogs. I was determined that I was going to make a difference. I was going to change the world.

And through it all, my family remained silent.
I'll never know how she infected my father and brothers, or why I was the only one to stand up to her. I'll never understand why she behaved the way she did, whether her actions were born of rage or indifference.
I only know that I survived, and I will continue to raise my voice.

20.
Heroes

You're disappointed, I can tell. It's fine, you don't have to pretend. Everybody is always disappointed. They've read all the stories and the news reports. They've seen the movie, and bought the whole 'happy ending', so they're expecting me to be off in Hollywood, rubbing shoulders with actors or models or some such.

Yeah, you didn't expect to find me in some crappy bar, two-thirds deep into a bottle of cheap whiskey. Gotta give you props though, kid, you came right up to me and spilled your guts anyway. It was obvious you'd been rehearsing – probably even practiced in front of the mirror a time or two. And I love that kind of bravery. It's the kind of bravery I used to have when I was your age. So, I'd love to help you find your brother, or sister, or lost dog. Whatever it was you were looking for. It's just that I'm not the person you think I am. I'm not the person I used to be before all that stuff happened to me.

I mean, all that pain, all that trauma? Nobody makes it out of that unscathed. Shit, kid. None of us get to be heroes in the end.

21.
Initiation

I was fifteen when I met him. Young and wild - and naïve. He introduced me to a world I never knew existed. A world that ran on threats and favours. A world of danger and excitement, where just living felt like getting away with something. Where each narrow escape only intensified the feeling that we were invincible, that nothing could bring us down.

He made it seem almost like a game. It started with skipping school, and lying to my parents. Then I moved on to selling colourful little pills - first to my friends and then, carefully, to strangers.

He introduced me to people - fun people, interesting people, and people that seemed to radiate danger. I learned first to navigate that world, and then to feel like I belonged. Even now, almost nothing can beat the rush of a nod from a dangerous man on the street.

I thought then that I would do anything for him. After all, I had already crossed so many lines. But the day he pressed a knife into my hands and, smiling, whispered about my 'initiation' was the day the scales fell from my eyes. I hadn't lost my mind after all, only temporarily misplaced it.

22.
Embers

Helen's bag was already packed when Ian came home. She jumped as she heard his key turn in the lock.

"What's this?" he demanded. "Are you going somewhere?"

She looked at her feet and remained silent.

"Well? Nothing to say?" He dropped the gym bag and took a step towards her.

Rage flared in her chest. "Yes, I have something to say. I'm leaving you. I've had enough of your anger and of your drinking. I'm not going to put up with it anymore." Her voice shook as she spoke, and she held her clenched fists at her sides.

He pointed at them. "You gonna hit me, are you? I've made you so mad that you're gonna try and punch me?"

She let out a breath and slowly unclenched her fists.

"No," she said.

"No," he repeated. "No, you're just gonna leave me. Well, go on then." He stood aside, leaving a clear path to the door. "Off you go."

Helen picked up her bag and threw it over her shoulder. Shaking, she moved past Ian. She was almost out of the door when he grabbed hold of her and dragged her back inside, shoving her so that she crashed into the wall and then slumped to the floor.

He slammed the door closed, and then turned and advanced on Helen, his own fists raised.

And when the worst of it was over, she found that she could still nurture the small, glowing embers of her rage, nestled in the ashes of her despair.

175

23.
Noisy Neighbours

Okay, apparently I have to keep this noise complaint record to 'prove' that there is a real issue with my next door neighbours, Tim and Leanne. I'm not sure how this will prove anything, but I'm willing to give anything a try at this point.

04:25 19th September – Woken by dog barking
They've left that poor dog alone all night, again. At least we managed to sleep until after four this time – the last time it barked for the whole night.

10:00 21st September – Neighbours had a fight
I could hear them screaming at each other for at least twenty minutes. Eventually, she told him that he's a 'useless sack of shit' and she threw him out. Again. We'll see how long it lasts this time before she lets him back in the house.
It's just a shame he didn't take the dog with him. I don't think they've walked it yet this week. Poor thing must be going stir crazy.

22:47 21st September – Tim banging on the door and shouting
I guess he didn't take too kindly to being turfed out. She must have taken his keys off him though – unless he just thought it would be more fun to try to kick the door in. Typical. I'd just managed to get to sleep, and I have to be up early in the morning.

07:03 24th September – Shouting and door slamming
Leanne was screaming at her daughter (Maisie or possibly Lacey, I can't quite tell), and it sounded like she was trying to kick down her door as well. I know the kid locks herself in her bedroom sometimes - I've heard Leanna shouting at her about it before. Anyway, she was yelling about how she has college on a Monday and the kid always makes her late.

College? What in the hell does she study?

17:48 27th September – Dog barking
The dog barked for about forty minutes, before Leanne came home and screamed at it to shut up.

19:02 30th September – Leanne screaming at the kids
It went on for a while, but I forgot to time it. The youngest boy went and sat outside on his own when it ended. I thought about saying something, but in the end I decided against it. I don't want to get involved; I just want them to stop waking me up.

07:50 6th October – Adults fighting
I don't know when she let him back in the house, but they're back to fighting again. I reckon it's going to end badly, she sounded scared today.

06:12 7th October – Dog barking
It's been barking all night. We called animal control and the lady who came out promised to do something about it, but it's the third time they've been out so I'm not holding my breath.

11:16 7th October – Screaming and dog barking

I must have fallen asleep sometime around seven. Leanne got home just before eleven. Usually her coming home shuts the dog up, but today it just went mad – barking and growling at her. And then she started screaming. I've never heard anything like it; she must have screamed for ten minutes solid.

They've both gone quiet now though.

24.
Squandered

No one sees me anymore. There was a time when I was young, and brave, and talented. When people took me seriously and asked for my advice. When they complimented me. When they wanted me.

But I didn't understand the currency of youth, and I squandered it on foolish things. On free drinks in grubby bars, bought by men who licked their lips, stared lasciviously and who weren't afraid to make demands, or to tell me all their squalid desires.

I didn't understand that the attention wouldn't last for ever, and I didn't spend it on the things that I should have. On getting ahead, making a name for myself, and getting out and into a place with more opportunity that my little, dead-end town.

It's taken me until now to realise that I want more for myself, to realise that I want my voice to ring out from the rooftops – right at the point that the world has decided that they're no longer prepared to listen.

So, I've made some poor choices. But I've seen – and understood – people who have done far worse things that I ever did, for the sake of someone just once looking them in the face and really seeing them.

25.
Loving

At five years old, you came to me in tears. Someone pushed you over in the playground. Silently seething, I soothed your hurt feelings and then, afterwards, I helped you to wash the dried blood from your knees.

At fifteen years old, you came to me, sheepishly. You were sticking up for a friend and you ended up getting into a fight in the park. Secretly proud, I listened to your story and then, afterwards, I helped you to clean the dried blood from your knuckles.

At twenty-five years old, you came to me and told me how someone hurt you in ways that I can't describe. Heartbroken, I helped you to bed. I soothed you while you fell asleep, but I didn't know how to put you back together. So, I did what any loving parent would. And then, afterwards, I washed the dried blood from my hands.

26.
The Safe-House

Claire woke suddenly with a pounding headache and sat bolt upright in bed. She was in a sparsely furnished room with only a couple of mattresses on the floor and a small cupboard in the corner. The early morning light was beginning to peek into the room from under an ill-fitting blind, which hung crookedly at the window.

She felt panic begin to rise in her chest. Before she had chance to move, a lump in the centre of the other mattress shifted, and a girl of about her own age sat up, pushing unruly brown curls out of her face.

"Calm down," the girl said, without preamble. "Nothing's going to happen to you here."

"I don't understand," Claire said.

The girl sighed. "You're in a safe-house," she began.

"What do you mean 'a safe-house'? Where am I?"

"Oh, I'm sorry, did you want an address? A grid reference? Should I break out a map and draw on it for you?"

Claire took a deep breath. "Okay, I get it. We're hidden. How did I get here?"

"Michael brought you in last night."

Claire frowned. A vague memory of a tall boy with a calm demeanour tugged at her consciousness.

"Why?"

The girl snorted. "You know why."

Claire stared at her. "You're like me."

"Wait." The girl held up one finger. Then she looked towards the door and called, "Come in, Michael."

The door opened and the tall boy entered, smiling nervously.

Claire felt her pulse rate increase.

"Stay there," the curly-haired girl said. "You're scaring her." And then, to Claire, "Will you please calm down. You're giving me a headache."

"I didn't say anything," Claire protested.

"You don't need to," Michael said. "Casey's an empath. She's picking up on your emotional state."

Claire turned to Casey, her eyes wide.

"What?" Casey snapped. "You thought all empaths would be doe-eyed 'tell me about your feelings' types? Do you have any idea how annoying it is having someone else's shit buzzing around in your head all the time?"

27.
The Assassins

He'd fought beside the assassins only once before. On the open battlefield they had seemed, at first, like anybody else. No better or worse than the men with whom he'd stood shoulder to shoulder for the last decade. It was only once they had fought their way inside that he began to see how they had earned their reputations. In close quarters, they ducked under swords, whirled, and slashed with their daggers, and then carried on down the halls, seemingly without pausing for breath.

When the battled was over and they were bloodied and victorious, he had taken a moment's pause from counting the dead in his own legion to nod to the leader of the assassins – a tall, scarred woman, with close-cropped hair – as she passed him. It had been the look in her eyes as much as her prowess on the battlefield that had made him breathe a sigh of relief that they were on the same side.

It had been almost three years since that night, but her face had stayed with him.

She was in the meeting with the other war-chiefs when he arrived. Her reputation must have elevated her over the years because when she spoke, which wasn't often, the others all listened.

"We will lead the incursion into the palace," she said.

"With the greatest of respect, Mistress, do you truly feel that your group should enter first, without protection from the soldiers?"

The man who had spoken was half concealed in the shadows at the back of the room. A hush followed his words.

"I do," the woman said, breaking the silence. "We already know the way. Many of us lived in the interior of the palace and we can show your men the safest route to the imperial chambers. Unless you would prefer to disarm the traps yourself, General?"

The traps at the palace were legendary. The general inclined his head and made no further comment.

He stood outside after the council meeting, as was his custom on the night before a battle. To his surprise, the woman joined him, appearing so suddenly beside him that it seemed she had materialised out of thin air.

"You have questions," she said, unprompted.

"You lived in the palace?" It seemed impossible.

"We were concubines."

"All of you?"

She nodded.

"And you just happened to all be skilled warriors?"

"Of course not." She stared at him with something like contempt. "Those of us who could not fight their way out of the palace died. Those of us who survived learned to be better." There was a moment's silence and then she said, "I hope you survive the coming battle. I should like to know you better."

"I hope we both survive it then," he said.

She smiled a grim smile. "There is no doubt in my heart that I will survive tomorrow. I have more motivation than most."

28.
Price of Admission

Dear Best Friend,

I could say that we've always been close, but that wouldn't be strictly true. The truth is that we've had times when we were like sisters, and times when we didn't want to know one another. That's normal, I think. There's a couple of years between us and that was enough of an age gap, when we were younger, that I had periods of finding you childish, and you had periods of finding me controlling. We grew up together though, and I never doubted that we would be in each other's lives, even when we fought.

And then you got married and had the kids.

Don't get me wrong, I like your husband very much and I love your kids. I love playing with them, pushing them on the swings, reading to them. I love the way their faces light up whenever they learn something new, or beat me at tag.

(Even though I'm pretty sure they know that I'm letting them beat me at tag.)

But somewhere along the way, it felt as if you forgot that there are other options.

All you ever talk about is kids. Your kids, your friends' kids (when did you turn into one of those people that start calling everybody so-and-so's mum or dad, by the way?). And you insist on talking about my imaginary future children.

Spoiler alert: There are no children in my future. I'm never going to be 'such-and-such's mother', I'm only ever going to be me. I know you think I'll change my mind - as if this is some kind of phase that I'll one day outgrow – but you're wrong. I don't need a husband or children to complete me; I'm a whole person already.

What would be nice though is if, just once in a while, you could ask me something about me. Because that's the price of admission to my life, a little pretence on your part that you value my choices the same way you value your own.

Sincerely, your best friend (who is never going to settle down)

29.
The Intern

"He promised." Matt gripped the arms of the chair until his knuckles turned white. "It was a key part of his campaign. It was why people voted for him. It was why I worked for him – for nothing – for the last two years."

The TV forgotten, his parents looked uneasily at each other.

His father cleared his throat. "It's a hard lesson to learn, son, but maybe it's best you learn it now. Politicians are all the same. They promise the earth when they're trying to get elected, but when it comes right down to it, they just don't deliver."

Matt rounded on him. "Maybe your generation let them get away with that, but mine won't."
"Let's not turn this into a generational thing," Matt's father began, but he was interrupted by Matt's mother, who had watched the argument with an ominous expression dawning across her face.
"Your generation? What are you going to do – go on the internet and whine about it? Sure, that'll show 'em! You act like you know better than us, as if you're so much more engaged, but we went to the marches, and joined the unions, and carried the damn signs at the protests, and you know what difference it made? None at all!"
"So, you just gave up?"

"Your mother is just being practical," Matt's father said, resting one hand lightly on his wife's arm. "There comes a time when you have to choose your battles."

Matt's shoulders slumped. "I did everything for him," he said. "I got in early to open up the office, I fixed his computer every time it broke. And for what? So he could lie to us all?"

"A hard lesson," his father repeated.

"Take the experience and do something useful with it," his mother said.

They turned the TV to a different channel, but Matt was no longer paying attention.

*What are you going to do?* his mother had said, *go on the internet and whine about it? Take the experience and do something useful with it, she'd said.*

Matt thought about the campaign office – about how it would be empty so late at night. About the passwords written on a post-it note, and stuck to the underside of a desk drawer.

He stood. "I think I'll go for a walk, to clear my head," he announced. "It shouldn't take long."

30.
Goddess of Vengeance

Euthalia checked the directions again and knocked on the door. It opened, swinging outwards so fast that it almost hit her.

"Are you...?" she trailed off, resisting the urge to use the word 'witch'.

The occupant of the house grinned a toothy grin and held out a small scrap of paper.

She hesitated. "Are you sure this will work?" she asked.

The woman nodded. "Everyone on your list will get what they deserve," she said.

Euthalia took the paper and dropped the coins in the woman's outstretched hand.

At home, she ground worm-wort and added it to the mixture in the small bowl lying in front of her. She threw in a handful of chicken bones, and then took a smouldering branch from the fire, holding it in the bowl just long enough for the contents to catch light. She jumped back as black smoke poured forth, filling the room.

Choking, she managed to get through the words of the spell. The smoke whirled and coalesced, finally forming itself into the figure of a woman.

"Adrasteia," Euthalia intoned. "Goddess of Vengeance, hear me. Bring to bear your great justice on my enemies here named."

She was about to start listing names, when the figure started to laugh. Her laughter rose until it filled the room, bouncing off the walls.

"Child, you have been misinformed," Adrasteia's voice was light and feminine. "I am not the goddess of vengeance, but the Goddess of Inescapable Fate. And in summoning me here today, you have set your own fate in motion."

Euthalia shrank back, her list of enemies forgotten. As the smoke travelled across the room to envelop her; as it poured into her open mouth, and down into her lungs, as the goddess' laughter rang in her ears, she had just enough time to curse the witch's name before everything went black.

# Part 5 -

# Joy

_____

1.
New Year's Gifts

It has long been Joanna's tradition to buy gifts for her friends and family at the turn of the new year. The gifts themselves are never expensive – it might be a notebook for her sister, Marie, or a scarf for her friend, Sam, but the items themselves are not the point.

There is a kind of magic that surrounds the beginning of anything new. It is a magic created from hope, from a desire for change, and it is never stronger than at this time of year, when the collective beliefs of thousands of people are all swirling through the aether.

Joanna siphons off a little of this magic and sprinkles it into her work, wrapping her hopes and dreams for her loved ones between the layers of brightly coloured tissue paper. She hums to herself as she fixes the last ribbon to the top of her pile of gifts.

Later she will deliver them to her unsuspecting family and friends, and they will exclaim in surprise over her generosity, while she smiles, and shrugs, and tells them each that she felt they deserved 'a little something extra' this year.

This too is part of the magic. None of them will remember that Joanna does the same thing every year. In fact, a few hours after they receive their gifts they will start to forget where they came from. But every time Marie writes in her notebook, or Sam wears his scarf, they will feel, for a few minutes at least, as if the world has become just a little bit brighter.

2.
A Birthday Message

"Happy Birthday, darling." My mother's voice makes me jump.

"Mum! How long have you been standing there?"

When I look closely, I realise that she's not so much standing as she is hovering, her feet vanishing into the coffee table. I make a move to clear it out of her way before I catch sight of the small frown on her face and remember just in time how much she hates people to 'make a fuss' over her spectral form. Instead, I plop myself down on the sofa and gesture for her to join me.

She smiles as she arranges herself, hovering just above the cushions, close enough that she looks like she's really sitting. It took her almost a year to master the trick and she loves to show it off whenever she can.

"Your grandma sends her love," she says, tucking her legs underneath her to complete the trick. "She wanted to come, but you know how she is about travel."

I nod. Grandma Iris had never even liked taking the number 4 bus, let alone making the journey from the astral plane.

"Was the traffic bad?" I ask, and my mother wrinkles her nose.

"Oh no worse than usual, I suppose. Although I swear the queues get worse every year." She reaches out and lays her hand across mine. I can't feel it, but I appreciate the gesture. "Although it was worth it to see you on your special day," she says, smiling.

(This story was originally published online under the

193

title 'A message from the other side' as part of National Flash Fiction Day's 'Flash Flood' 2021)

3.
Multitudes

I was too empty for words, too empty for anything to reach me, let alone touch me.

But then you took me by the hand and showed me how to walk through your mind, how to share your dreams.

I had never seen anything like it. Where my mind had slipped into greyscale, yours was bursting with colour. It was as if I had tumbled into a living painting; everywhere I looked there was vibrancy and life. Whole galaxies swirled above my head, their purples and blues dotted with pinpricks of white and silver light. Jungles flourished at my feet in an array of calming greens and tropical oranges and pinks.

"Look anywhere," you said, your voice seeming to echo through my own mind. "Nothing here is off limits."

You've been gone for years now. I like to think about you from time to time, out there, somewhere, happy. But even though you're gone, your gift is still with me. I only have to close my eyes and I can see the colours, still.

4.
Angels in the Garden

I don't get to see my niece as often as I'd like. When she was born I promised myself that I would be her 'Cool Aunty', someone who she could come to when she was a kid so I could spoil her, and someone who she could come to when she was a teenager so she could complain about her mum. Every teenage girl needs a safe place to complain about their mum, after all.

But it didn't quite work out like that. I travelled a lot for the first few years of her life and even when I was at home, my working hours hadn't been exactly what you might call 'kid friendly'. So, I've become not so much her 'Cool Aunt' as her aunt who turns up once in a blue moon but usually brings presents.

But I have a new job now, with new hours, so all that is about to change. Starting with looking after Emma for the day so that her mum can get some much needed 'me' time.

"Are you sure about this?" my sister asks looking dubiously at my pastel-coloured décor.

"Of course," I say brightly. "We're going to have loads of fun, aren't we, Em?"

It's hard to say which of the two of them looks more sceptical.

"Can I play in the garden?" Emma asks, when her mother finally leaves.

"Yes you can. How about if I make us some squash and we'll have a picnic?"

"You need food for a picnic, Aunty Kay," Emma tells

me solemnly.

"Well then I'll just have to bring some cookies too," I say, watching her face light up.

She runs off and I add orange squash to a jug of water, careful not to make it too strong (according to my sister's instructions). I'm just about to grab the cookies, when I look up to see Emma lying on her back in one of the flowerbeds with her arms and legs outstretched, making what I can only describe as 'mud angels'.

"Emma!" I shout. "Come here and let me clean that off!"

In response, she pulls a face and dashes away.

I should be angry but something about it strikes me as so comical that I double over laughing. I laugh so hard that it's all I can do to give chase as she capers around the garden, the happiest I've ever seen her.

5.

The Case of the Disappearing Demon

Baines and I were only ever called up from Hell on the most fiendishly difficult of cases. And none of our investigations were ever trickier than the 'Case of the Disappearing Demon'.

It seems that one of the denizens of the Underworld had become a bit bored with tormenting lost souls and had gone for a jaunt topside. This was something that happened every now and again - eternity is an awfully long time to be stuck in the same job after all. But it was the damnedest thing with this one; try as we might, we just couldn't find him. The blighter must have taken over a human (fairly common practice) and then developed a real skill for blending in (most uncommon amongst our kind).

Baines and I finally got a whiff of some demonic activity at some kind of mortal health spa in the far reaches of North America. We took possession of two of the guests and proceeded to avail ourselves of the facilities – health treatments, tennis lessons, cold water swimming sessions, that sort of thing. Actually, I quite enjoyed the latter. But I digress.

"Any luck?" I asked Baines as we passed in the lobby.

"Dining room, eight o'clock tonight," he replied. "All shall be revealed."

He always did have a penchant for the dramatic.

We were seated at our table by seven. It meant an hour of tedium while we forced ourselves to eat tasteless human food and make pointless human small talk. Demons are not well versed in small talk. The weather, for example, is an infrequent topic of conversation in Hell, what with there being very little in the way of variety.

The time did at least afford us the opportunity to observe the other occupants of the spa. Besides ourselves there were a handful of other guests, all aged around the same age as the bodies we had inhabited, which is to say 'old' by human standards. There was the tennis instructor, who seemed to be in the habit of carrying a sports bag with him at all times, the swimming teacher, who had changed into an evening gown that she no doubt thought was flattering, and various members of the wait-staff, who moved nimbly from one table to another, balancing various trays and plates in a way I found almost pleasing to watch.

"Well," Baines said. "What do you think?"

I considered each of the humans in turn. There did seem to be a hint of something slightly sulphurous in the air, but damned if I could tell where it was coming from.

"Give up?" Baines asked, a note of triumph in his voice. "That's our quarry, right there!" He leapt to his feet, overturning his chair in the process, and pointed at the tennis instructor.

As I said, dramatic.

The man Baines had accused wasted no time but stood and ran for the door. I gave chase and managed to tackle him just before he reached the lobby.

"But how did you know the tennis instructor was the demon?" I asked, struggling to hold onto him as he reverted back to his real form.

"Simplicity itself, my dear chap," Baines replied. He

picked up the sports bag and unzipped it, showing me the contents. "No one else could possibly have wielded the infernal racquet."

6.
The Train

I used to have a recurring dream whenever I was anxious. As a child, it would happen whenever my parents fought, as a teenager, it would surface around exam time, and as an adult, much to my shame, it would happen whenever there was any conflict at work.

The dream was always the same. I was the only passenger on a runaway train as it barrelled towards a solid brick wall. I would wake, sometimes screaming and always in a cold sweat, just before it crashed.

I was so troubled by the dream, which had begun to occur almost every night, that I went to see a specialist.

"Tell me all about it," he said. "In detail," he added, after I gave him the briefest possible version. "Every sound, every smell. As much as you can remember."

I described the train, an old blue steam train like something out of a child's cartoon. I told him how it rushed down the track, gathering pace until the trees on either side were nothing but a blur.

"And the wall?" he asked.

"Old. Dirty." I frowned. "Covered in graffiti."

"And what does the graffiti say?"

I closed my eyes and tried to picture it, but the words seemed to smudge into nonsense.

"Take your time," he said.

I took deep breaths and concentrated, and, after a few moments, the nonsense began to coalesce back into words.

"Divorce," I read, a note of triumph in my voice. "Failure."

"Do these words in particular mean anything to you?"

"They're the things I used to be afraid of when I was a child. My parents getting divorced, me failing my exams." I opened my eyes. "The wall represents my fears?"

"Very good," he said, smiling. "So now that we know, we're going to try an exercise to deal with this, okay?"

"Okay."

He reached out and put one cool, dry hand against my forehead.

"Stay on the train," he said.

The world went black and when I opened my eyes, I was standing on the train, the trees and bushes rushing past outside.

I ran to the cabin and saw the wall approaching.

The words 'stay on the train' held me there, even as part of my brain was screaming at me, *"I can't! If I stay, I'll hit the wall, I'll derail, I'll die!"*

Instead, with the scream of the train whistle ringing in my ears, I rode the train as it punched right through the wall, landing safely on the other side.

7.
Reasons to Stay

Ed had always talked a good fight about wanting to leave, but when it came right down to it he always found a reason to stay. College was too expensive, or the economy was bad, or his parents were getting older and would need someone to look after them.

But one by one, his reasons began to disappear. He was too old to go to college, the economy was just as bad in his small town as it was everywhere else. And then his parents did the unthinkable, they upped sticks and moved away down south.

"We want to be somewhere warmer," his dad said.

Apparently, they weren't going to be told that they were old and needed someone to take care of them.

So, Ed revisited all his old plans, his fantasies of moving away to the big city, or to any place where things happened and where they might actually happen to him.

He stood outside his family home, a few weeks after he'd waved his parents off with plenty of promises of mutual phone calls and visits on both sides. It seemed to him now as if the place itself didn't want him to leave. The grass, long and wild, seemed to catch at his ankles, as if it would have held him there if it could. But his mind was, finally, made up. He took one last look and then kicked away the grasping weeds, breaking the chains of his past as he took his first steps towards his future.

8.
A Captive Audience

"How did we end up here?" the Paladin asked, from inside the cage.

The Archer sighed, resting her arms against the thick wooden bars of her small prison cell. "No point asking me, I told you we would need to stop to buy more arrows. It's not my fault you didn't listen when we had the chance."

"What's the point of you if you're useless every time we run out of arrows?" asked the Rogue, picking at his fingernails as he spoke.

"Me, useless? What about her?" the Archer pointed at the next cell, where the Sorceress dangled, upside-down and gagged, from a makeshift beam along the ceiling.

The Sorceress made a muffled sound into her gag that was, presumably, meant as a protest.

"Quiet, everyone. He's back," the Paladin said.

Three of the party watched as the Ogre approached. The Sorceress had accidentally spun round and was forced to stare at the back wall of her cell.

The Ogre looked them all over, cleared his throat, and then launched into a long and mostly incomprehensible story involving a hunting party, a unicorn, and a group of trolls.

"...And then he went 'splat'!" he finished, bringing his fist down on a table and laughing riotously. After a moment he seemed to realise his captives had remained silent and he glared at them until they too laughed. Nervously.

"Humour is relative, after all," reasoned the Rogue.

9.

The Power of Sharing

You had been sick for months and it was obvious, despite your protests, that you were getting worse, but still, somehow, I wasn't expecting the news when it came.

"He's gone," Claire said, and her words seemed to explode like dynamite, a searing flash of white that bleached all the colour from the world.

And we were silent in our grief. We couldn't find the words to explain what you had meant to us.

But then, one by one, we started to speak.

Katherine poured wine and told us the story of how you'd once got so animated telling a story at dinner that you had sent a glass of red wine flying across the table, covering everyone who'd been sitting opposite you.

We all began to imitate the way you used to talk with your hands, the expansive gestures you would make to illustrate whatever story you happened to be engaged in telling at the time.

Damien talked about that evening in Portugal when you had persuaded us all to go swimming in the sea at sunset.

"Come on," he mimicked. "The sun's been shining all day. It'll be -"

"- Like a hot tub!" we all finished in unison, laughing.

"And then it was freezing cold!" Katherine said.

"And we had to walk back past all the locals, soaking wet," Claire said.

"And they were all shaking their heads at us for being so stupid." I was laughing so hard I could hardly talk.

A trickle of stories became a stream and then a torrent. And each memory we shared brought a little bit of colour back into the world.

10.
Ostara's Song

Ostara woke after a long sleep. Yawning, she raised herself up from her winter bed of bracken and purple heather. It seemed to her that she had dreamed of wild winds and of the grey, rolling seas. Of heavy snows that blanketed the land until barely a trace of life remained visible, save for the red berries of the holly bush, bright against the glowing whiteness.

She crept from her resting-place, pleased to see that the traces of winter were already beginning to give way under her feet. As she walked through the world, she felt the cool night breeze dance along her bare arms, raising goosebumps on her flesh as it passed. The stars glittered sharply overhead, and when she breathed in, there was a hint already of something green in the air. It seemed the world was waiting, in the space before the dawn. Waiting to wake up.

As she walked, she began to sing. The sky turned pink and then blue above her, and the ground began to warm where the sun's bright rays swept across it. Beneath the surface of the earth, seeds started to stretch and unfurl, becoming shoots and then flowers. Her song rose and soared, waking the birds so that they added their voices to her own, carrying the song with them as they travelled. And in this way, spring returned to the land.

11.
The Kitten

Fiona had noticed the kitten in the garden a few times. It was a scrawny little thing with no collar and nothing to suggest that anyone was looking for it. There were no notices appealing for its safe return and, when she spoke to her neighbours, none of them knew anything about it.

She started buying cat food almost on a whim. She left bowls of it outside, along with fresh water, before leaving for work in the morning. When she returned the water was usually untouched, but the food was almost always gone.

As the days passed, the kitten began to spend more time in the garden, and to venture closer to the house.

Fiona took to buying toys for him - a soft mouse, a fish on a string attached to a plastic fishing rod. This last was the most successful; she found that the kitten would be so entranced with it that he would let her almost close enough to touch before he would dash away, his eyes wide. Fiona resolved to think of a way to lure the kitten inside, where she could check him over properly and feed him.

She knew the storm was coming hours before it arrived. She kept watch anxiously at the window, but there was no sign of the kitten.

She stood in the garden, umbrella in hand, as the rain began to fall and, just as she was about to give up and go indoors, she heard a mewling sound coming from behind the shed. She followed the sound until she found him, scrunched up tight in the space between the shed and the fence.

It took several minutes to coax him out, and longer to persuade him inside. When Fiona finally got him to settle - his icy paws padding at her knee - his purring almost drowned out the storm.

12.
Reinvention

"It's a small town," I tell myself, "With a small super-market. It doesn't mean anything if I see the same people when I go shopping."

Except it's not the same 'people', it's the same person. One person. A tall man with thick glasses and a beard, who seems to be everywhere I go.

He was buying ice cream as I walked down the frozen food aisle on Tuesday (strawberry ice cream, one of the cheaper brands). He was checking the ripeness of the avocados as I added oranges to my basket on Friday. And when I walked through the doors on Monday morning, there he is again, browsing through the magazines.

He doesn't speak to me, but there is something in the way he looks at me, something in the way his eyes move over my face, almost as if he is measuring me against an image in his mind, that tells me it's time for me to make my move.

I duck down the bakery aisle where, I hope, he won't think to follow me, and circle back to the door. There's no sign of him as I leave and, although I take a circuitous route, and double back on myself a couple of times, he doesn't follow me home.

I take a moment to look around my little house, at the bright splash of yellow paint on the dining room walls, and the roses growing in a pot in the kitchen window. I don't need long. I'm good at this by now.

I clear the house, wipe away the traces of this identity, prepare to move on. I managed almost three years of peace this time, but truth be told, I was beginning to get a little bored anyway. And there are worse things than a little reinvention.

I smile. I wonder who I'll be next.

13.
Drastic Measures

Abigail regarded the boy out of the corner of her eye, trying to hide the fact that she was watching him. He wasn't much to look at, skinny and soaking wet, as he shivered under a blanket. He was young too – no more than fourteen, she guessed. That was young to be chosen for a quest of this magnitude, even by the Order of Vyryne's standards. Still there was something about him, something shining in his aura that spoke to her of a kind of inner strength.

"You are afraid?" she asked, not unkindly.

The boy looked her full in the face, as if he was noticing her for the first time. Unlike her, he didn't bother to hide his scrutiny.

"Yes," he said. Shame rushed through him as he spoke, but there was no trace of it in his voice and very little evidence of it on his face. He had been well trained to conceal his emotions. "I don't want to fail."

"Of course not," she replied.

It was more than that though, she could sense it. Desolation seemed to roll off the boy in waves, as if he had already decided his quest was doomed. Clearly, he was going to need some help.

She stood and crossed the floor briskly, opened a small cabinet and rifled through the contents until she found what she was looking for, a clear bottle labelled 'Hope'. She took it out and paused for a moment, admiring the way the clear liquid inside shimmered as it caught the light. She poured a generous measure into a teacup and handed it over.

"Drink," she said.

As the boy drained the cup, he felt his courage return, his possibilities expand.

"Can I have another?" he asked.

She shook her head. "That's enough to get you started. The rest is up to you."

14.
The Reindeer

Sophie has been trying to fall asleep for what feels like hours. Every time she closes her eyes, she seems to see strings of fairy lights sparkling against the darkness and she imagines she can hear the echo of carollers as they make their way through the streets.

Sophie has only been living in her new house for a few weeks and she is worried that Santa won't be able to find them to deliver her presents.

"I sent my letter before we moved," she told her brother, Michael, earlier. "How will he know where we are now?"

"Magic, Soph," Michael had replied, wiggling his fingers at her.

She sighs now, unconvinced, and turns over in bed, dragging the covers with her. Sophie is just beginning to feel herself drifting off when she hears a noise outside. She stands on the bed, trying her hardest to see out of the window, but there's nothing there.

Undeterred, she runs to Michael's room and shakes him awake.

"I heard a reindeer outside! It's Santa!"

"There's no -" he begins and then stops. "Come on then," he says instead, sighing. "Let's go see."

She follows him outside and they both stare at the hoofprints that lead down the garden path and then vanish suddenly, leaving nothing but the snow drifting softly through the night.

15.
The Dancer in the Dark

Nicola stepped out from under the canopy of trees, blowing on her hands to warm them.

"How're you doing?" she asked Adrian.

"Ready for the show," he replied.

Nicola squinted at the sky. "I think the clouds should blow over soon," she said.

The two of them spread a blanket on the ground and huddled together on top of it.

"You've seen the lights before, right?" Adrian asked.

"A few times. My family used to come up here when I was a kid. My dad used to tell me all the stories about them."

"What stories?" Adrian shifted, settling into a more comfortable position.

"There's all sorts. The Norse used to think they were watching a battle, and the aurora were lights reflecting off the fighters' shields. The Romans used to think it was the goddess of the dawn driving her chariot across the sky. But my favourite story was the one that we made up ourselves." She let out a self-conscious little laugh.

"Tell me."

"I used to imagine that it was a lady in a long, green ball gown, sweeping across the floor. I called her 'the dancer in the dark' when I was little."

"I like that," he said, smiling. "I can just see you as a kid, telling your folks all about your 'dancer'."

He wrapped his arms around her, and they both watched, in silence, as the lights appeared in the sky.

16.
Peace (and Quiet) to All

Family Christmas looks a little different this year.

"It's fine," Dad assures me over Zoom. "Your mum and I are quite enjoying the peace and quiet."

We chat for a while and open our presents on camera, oohing and aahing over the socks and scarves, dropped off on our respective doorsteps the week before.

From somewhere behind them I hear a loud beeping.

"Oops, that'll be the oven timer," Mum says. "Time to put on the stuffing. Or was it the carrots first?"

From the kitchen, I can hear the tell-tale sounds of pots and pans starting to be pushed aside.

Dad winks at me. "We best get things back on track here, love," he says.

"That's ok, I promised I'd chat with Jenny before lunch anyway. Enjoy your peaceful Christmas," I say, doing that awkward Zoom wave thing, as I try to hang up.

I manage it on the third stab at the screen and, once I'm sure I'm not still somehow connected to my parents' living room, I dial my sister.

She picks up on the third ring. "Merry Christmas!" she shouts. "Boys come here and wish your Aunty Erin happy Christmas!"

I can hardly hear her over all the noise in the background.

"Noah!" she shouts, looking just off camera. "Stop that!"

In the corner of the screen, the Christmas tree wobbles ominously.

"Got your hands full there," I say.

"They're a gift," she says through gritted teeth. "A blessing."

17.
Christmas Traditions

"Okay," said Tommy, in a tone his family have come to recognise as his 'announcing' voice. "I love Christmas -"

"Obviously," Billy cut in.

"Hush, Billy," Mother said. "Go on, Tommy."

"I love Christmas. I love all of you -"

"What, no 'obviously' this time?" Dad asked, earning himself a glare from across the table. He made a zipping motion across his mouth.

" – and I love coming to Grandma's for Christmas," Tommy continued, undeterred. "But I don't get why we have to eat these … things." He poked at a pile of sprouts with his fork.

"Yes, why is that?" asked Dad, frowning at his own pile of sprouts.

"It's a Christmas tradition," said Grandma. "And it's always been a rule in this family. Everyone has to eat at least two sprouts with their dinner."

"But they're gross," Tommy said.

"They're good for you. And if you stop making such a fuss and just eat them it'll be over before you know it. Look, Billy has eaten his already and you didn't hear him complaining, did you?"

Billy exchanged a conspiratorial look with the dog.

18.
Endless Possibilities

The thought struck her suddenly that every person in the world probably made a hundred decisions a day that changed the course of their lives in some small way. Not just the obvious decisions - do I get married, change jobs, move house, have kids? But the small ones that no one thinks about. Turn left instead of right, stay home instead of going out. Order white wine that night instead of red. A hundred, thousand tiny little changes that splinter off down different paths, that all affect the course of our lives.

As someone who suffered from anxiety, the thought should have been terrifying. The idea that there are just too many variables for any one person to really control the direction of their lives. Instead, for some strange reason, she found the idea exhilarating. All those tiny decisions. All those possibilities. The endless versions of herself she created at every turn. Here, a woman who stayed home drinking red wine. Here, a version of herself who met the love of her life pressed up against a wall at a party. There, a woman living quietly in the country or alone in an apartment in New York City. So many lives. So many equally possible, equally valuable, equally well reasoned lives. Almost as if she couldn't go wrong.

19.
Golden Threads

This is why I love coming to restaurants by myself; nothing else gives me such a great opportunity for people-watching. Take the couple at the table next to me, now. They've clearly been together for a while, and they're past that 'gazing lovingly into one another's eyes' stage of the relationship, but I can see that the first blooms of their infatuation have deepened into something stronger. The strong, golden thread stretching between them tells me everything I need to know.

They have other threads of course, everybody does, and if I wanted to, I could pick anybody in here, take any thread and follow it back to someone in their lives; a mother, a brother, even someone less significant like an old schoolfriend.

The stronger and brighter the thread, the more significant the relationship. And the couple in front of me shine so brightly that it comes as no surprise to me when he draws the small, velvet box from inside his jacket pocket.
I turn away, smiling, and find someone else to watch.

(This story was originally published online as part of National Flash Fiction Day's 'Flash Flood' 2021)

20.
The Sound of 2 A.M.

Strange isn't it, how music can act almost as a snapshot, fixing a picture in your mind of the first time you learned a song, or the first time you danced to it. An everlasting image of the meaning you ascribed to the notes the first time you heard them played.

We're old souls, you and I. We've lived through changing fashions and the moments when everything comes back around again, recycled into new and fascinating fractals.

But there's a certain type of jazz music that transports me back a hundred years. To nights spent half drunk on love and whiskey. To clubs where the smoke hangs in the air, obscuring the realities and leaving only tantalizing possibilities dancing in front of our eyes. To the sound of 2 A.M. To you.

21.
The Jump

"You going to do it?" Shaun asked each of them. "Jamie? You up for it, mate?"

Jamie nodded, his heart in his throat.

Shaun grinned. "Trust me. It'll be amazing."

Jamie watched as his friend teased and cajoled the rest of the group. Some of them took more convincing than others but eventually they all stood in a small, nervy huddle, waiting for the signal.

"Ready?" Shaun asked. "Three ... two ... one - go!"

Jamie ran with the others, his heart pounding. As he reached the edge of the rock he pushed off, tucking his legs underneath him the way Shaun had shown them.

For a long moment he had the sense that he wasn't really falling, that he was just hanging in the empty air, but then he began to drop. The sea seemed to rise up to meet him, and he plunged into the cool water.

He found himself completely submerged, surrounded by bubbles that danced across his skin. As he pushed up, he broke the surface of the water, heaving in a great lungful of air. Around him, he could see his friends all doing the same.

"I told you!" Shaun whooped, slapping Jamie on the shoulder. "Didn't I tell you it was great!"

Jamie grinned back, too happy – and relieved – to reply.

22.
The Art of Kitchen Procrastination

"Okay, you have two options. You either do your chores, right now, like we agreed, or the cinema trip is off."

"Fine," Ethan grumbled. "I'll do them."

Karen nodded, despite clearly wanting to say more. Ethan stuck his tongue out as she left, just managing to pull his face back into a smile as she spun round. He blinked innocently and she finally departed, her lips twisted with suspicion.

Okay, chore number one, Ethan checked the list pinned up on the fridge. Empty the dishwasher. Ugh. Boring.

He pulled the cutlery container from the dishwasher and began to empty it into a drawer.

*Fork, spoon, knife. Fork, spoon ... hey what if I was a swordfighter but I only used the world's smallest swords.*

Ethan pinched a butter knife between his thumb and forefinger and waved it around, picturing himself duelling tiny opponents.

Karen appeared in the doorway. "What are you doing?"

Ethan coughed. "The, um, knife was still wet. I was just drying it."

"Get on with it, Ethan."

"I am!"

Karen vanished out of sight.

Grumbling, Ethan picked up a plate.

*Hey*, he thought, *what if I was a ninja but I only used*

*the world's biggest throwing stars?*

Without thinking, he made a throwing motion. The plate slipped from his grasp, flew across the room, and crashed against the wall, shattering into pieces.

"Ethan!" Karen yelled. "Did you just throw one of my plates at the wall? What on earth are you doing? You're thirty-seven years old!"

(This story was originally written for Round 1 of NYC Midnight's 'Microfiction 250' Challenge 2021)

# Acknowledgements

Thank you so much to my Mum and Dad, Anna, Mike, Elliott and Marcus, Paula, Debs, David, Sophie and Megan, Jo, Craig and Laura, Gillie and Hatts and all at HDP, and my friends in the vss community.

Thank you most of all to John.

# About the author

Amy Wilson is a writer and editor from Teesside, in north-east England. She has written short stories for the 'Harvey Duckman Presents' anthologies in the UK and for 3Moon Magazine and the 'From One Line' anthologies in the USA, as well as contributing stories to the No Sleep Podcast, and to National Flash Fiction Day's 'Flash Flood' event.

She was nominated for an award for her microfiction story, 'The Colour of Darkness' in summer 2021, and is one of the founding editors of 'Word Salad' magazine.

Printed in Great Britain
by Amazon

69742398R00139